ROOM 502

ROOM 502

FIRST CINEVISTA EDITION

Kevin Alyn Elders

Cinevista
Screen Novel Series ™
Los Angeles & Villefranche Sur Mer
2015

Cinevista, Inc
A Screen Novel ™
www.KevinAlynElders.com

ISBN-13: 978-1-943673-01-8
ISBN-10: 1943673012

The Cataloging-in-Publication Data is on file at Library of Congress

Manuscript Services by
Rogena Mitchell-Jones
www.rogenamitchell.com

Cover Designed By Kristin Designs
kristindesign100@gmail.com

The *Leone di San Marco* photographed & designed by K.A.Elders

"No film can equal the narrative attack of *ROOM 502*… Brilliant storytelling... Spellbinding entertainment from a truly gifted American writer …"

— *Albert S. Ruddy, Academy Award Winning Producer of 'The Godfather' & 'Million Dollar Baby'*

Contents

ACKNOWLEDGEMENTS

I've been a working screenwriter for three decades and I've been blessed to have the privilege of working with some of the giants of the motion picture industry. Over the years, many of them have urged me to turn my screenplays into novels. I resisted, but it occurred to me that if I applied the same hard-fought brevity to writing novels that I apply to writing screenplays, perhaps a more concise, compelling form of literature could emerge that would captivate the reader without requiring so much chair time. Hence, the *Screen Novel Series* was born—stories imagined as movies but written as literature for the cinema inside your head. I hope you'll enjoy the journey and I am immensely grateful for your time.

For my Father,
Whoever you are
Wherever you are
I wish I could have known you

Prologue

"Venice is the only city in the world where lions fly and pigeons walk."

—*Jean Cocteau*

But tonight, the pigeons were flying. Even in the rain. Their wings fluttered in a downpour that battered centuries-old limestone and the intoxicated carnival goers stumbling across it.

Carnival time and an icy February deluge were the perfect cover for the murder about to take place. A time when alcohol flowed harder in tourists' veins than the midnight tide flowed in Venetian canals. A time when masks obscured intent and the telltale signs of an evil ready to strike.

The pigeons sensed the menace as it waited. They flocked toward it, landing on ancient cupolas eager to be its witness. Perhaps the abject boredom of scavenging crumbs from the hands of small children made the pigeons hungry for real action. The kind that took place in the fog-filled porticos of the fish market near the Rialto where they witnessed a wobbly stiletto heel splashing into a puddle of fish blood gurgling down a drain.

As the fragile footwear bounded past, they noticed it belonged to a woman in a trench coat clutching a yellow umbrella. She moved quickly through the deserted market to escape the tempest. She was oblivious to the white mask watching her from the shadows.

She finally spotted the masked voyeur as she passed the portico where he lingered. She didn't seem afraid. It was carnival week in Venice and such occurrences were common. She turned into a narrow calle and went on her way.

The costumed voyeur slipped from the shadows to follow her, the pelting rain masking the sound of his footsteps. Still, the woman sensed something. She turned nervously and caught sight of him ducking back into a doorway. She started to run. A mistake in the rain. She paid for it dearly, slipping on a tile.

In an instant, he was upon her. With an almost operatic flurry, his cloak swept the air to conceal his prey. She kicked frantically as he forced a clear plastic bag over her head and wound a leather cord around her neck.

As he jerked it taut, she gagged violently and knocked the mask from his face. The killer turned away quickly as his veil of anonymity fluttered to the ground.

The mask came to rest calmly on the rain-soaked limestone until the victim's lifeless body collapsed on top of it.

Lightning flashed in the distance and the pigeons flew away.

Chapter I

The Grand Canal is nothing if not a dichotomy. For centuries, its serpentine swathe has bisected a city-state in perpetual decay. A begrudging host to gondolas, galleons, prisoners, and kings, its surface has been the subject of countless masterpieces, yet the endless current of human excrement flowing beneath it has remained invisible to the eye. And thankfully, in winter at least, the other senses as well.

That winter evening, one of Venice's legendary sunsets threatened to take place. The previous night's rain had fled to the Adriatic leaving a corduroy sky in its wake awash with salmon cumulus worthy of a Canaletto.

From balustrades high above the Grand Canal, a man holding a half-empty wine glass eyed another dichotomy as it bobbed through the lazy maritime traffic below.

He watched a classic wooden Venetian Motoscafo listing to starboard as it lumbered through choppy waters burdened by a bizarre and unexpected cargo—two ornate antique mirrors, a brass floor lamp, and the beast of the litter—*an intricately carved armoire.*

All pieces were in exquisite condition, as was the single passenger chaperoning them— Claudia Bellini shielded her lily-white face from the sun. Her long blonde hair was hidden under a red hat. Her bright blue eyes were shielded by dark designer glasses. Every curve of her body was wrapped in an almost suffocating tightness by a cadmium red suit. She was the stuff of men's dreams, and the massive diamonds on her fingers proved those dreams costly.

Claudia anxiously eyed an imposing five-story sixteenth century palazzo at the edge of the Grand Canal. The Palazzo Giovanni was a standout amongst the many ancient villas converted into intimate Venetian hotels. Host to countless doges and their mistresses in centuries past, a sanctuary of discretion for the wealthy and the privileged, it was now the destination for a beautiful woman and her mysterious cargo.

The driver of Claudio's motoscafo eased the vessel to port, gently nudging the landing of the Giovanni's side entrance. Three porters streamed toward them from inside.

Giuseppe Rossini, the hotel manager, trailed behind them rushing to greet his pedigreed guest. Rossini was typically Venetian, sporting a waxed moustache and toothy grin.

"Buon giorno, Signora Bellini!" Rossini gushed. "The soul of the humble house of Giovanni has been mourning your absence."

Claudia eyed him dismissively. "Spare me the poetics, Rossini. I couldn't bear spending another night with pieces in such pathetic condition."

Claudia's accent was Italian. Her manner clipped, contemptuous of Rossini's effusive style. Rossini marveled at the antiques as a porter nearly slipped into the canal off-loading the cumbersome armoire. Claudia chastised the errant porter in Italian. Rossini followed with a slap to the man's temple.

"I'm so sorry, signora!" he apologized as he motioned her inside. "They look magnificent. The restoration must have cost you a fortune."

"It cost me nothing," she answered dryly. "You can thank my husband."

"But, of course," he groveled. "And how is Signor Bellini?"

"I wouldn't know. Ask his mistress."

Claudia disappeared into the ornately carved doorway of the hotel. Rossini, slightly embarrassed, followed closely behind.

Once inside, she headed for the large seventeenth century desk dominating a lobby embellished with architectural elegance. No guests were in evidence. Intimacy and privacy seemed to be the convention. Rossini signaled two more porters to assist with her antique *cargo*.

"Would you like them placed in your room now, signora or—?"

"Of course *now*," she answered as she eyed the porters with disdain. "Otherwise, these assassins of yours will destroy them."

Rossini stiffened dutifully. "At once, signora!" He indicated a stately marble stairway and barked at a frazzled porter. "Room 502. Andiamo… Andiamo!"

The porters snapped to it. Rossini handed Claudia a key attached to a gondola shaped fob elegantly engraved with the number *502*.

"May I offer you a complimentary meal in our dining salon this evening, signora?" he asked sheepishly.

"The food in your dining salon is anything but *complimentary*. I'll dine in my room. See to it I'm not disturbed."

She grabbed the key impatiently and turned as Rossini nodded subserviently. He secretly despised her, yet he, along with everyone else, couldn't take their eyes off her sensual hips as her high heels negotiated the staircase winding toward the rooms above.

IN THE GIOVANNI'S upper portego, light streamed off the Grand Canal through etched Venetian windows as the porters jockeyed the antiques through a doorway.

Claudia monitored them carefully as a *dark-haired chambermaid* passed by. The two exchanged a smile. One might have sensed it was more than that, but perhaps it was just the Palazzo working its spell.

The Giovanni was a mysterious place, enchanting, much like the city herself. Gilded ceilings, spidery chandeliers, and paintings whose subjects brazenly followed you with their eyes. Claudia seemed uniquely at home there.

The porters finished. She tipped them generously and moved inside, shutting the door behind her. As it closed, it revealed the numerical wedges of polished bronze staking claim to the room—*502*.

Once inside, Claudia latched both locks before turning to luxuriate in a vision that would have impressed even the most cynical of

Royals. Room 502 was simply magic. A large, canopied Florentine bed dominated her view but quickly gave way to the extraordinary stone fireplace in front of it. Massive paintings of doges past. Ceilings jeweled in mosaic. Every fabric was a spectacle. Every sculpture a subject worth study. The armoire now stood at its rightful place among them.

Claudia was a sucker for the magic. She soaked it all in, and then opened two delicate glass doors and walked out onto a stunning tiled terrace covered with sculptures of topiary and stone. A soft canvas canopy shielded her from the crimson glow of the setting sun as she wove her way toward the balustrades at its edge.

Claudia arrived to a view kings had mounted campaigns to claim. The bell tower of St. Mark's in the background. A wall of noble palaces in the foreground, and the enchanting host to the gondola and vaporetto five stories beneath her—the Grand Canal.

A breeze kicked up off the water. Claudia seemed mesmerized by it. She massaged her body as if she were naked using the wind as oil. Her mouth tightened as her hands rubbed her clothing sensually. First, her waist, then her hips, then suddenly—a voice.

"In the interest of my sanity, I better interrupt you."

Claudia spun around finding the man with the wine glass, who had been watching her from above as she arrived earlier. He was seated off to the side at a small table. As he stood up, Claudia was still startled but showed no sign of embarrassment.

The tall American intruder had a manner women found hard to ignore. Dark hair, grey-blue eyes. He was dressed impeccably in an elegant Italian suit. He was intrigued but unfazed by her presence.

"Jack Sands. I'm sorry if I startled you."

Jack extended his hand. Claudia shook it reticently.

"Are you lost, Mr. Sands?"

"Now that's a loaded question," he answered wryly. "You mean am I in the wrong room?"

"I know you're in the wrong room. I'm just curious how you got here?"

"I spent the last two nights here. I was only staying for the sunset. If you'd like me to leave …"

"Not at all," Claudia interrupted. "How could I deny you?"

She moved back toward the room calmly.

Jack suddenly realized the best view in Venice was walking away from him. As she headed to the door of the terrace, she called out without turning.

"Do you like grappa, Mr. Sands?"

"Depends on the grappa," he answered, standing to follow her.

"Picolit. 1985."

"Pretty potent stuff for a lady," Jack noted surprised.

She stopped briefly and turned toward him, her thin smile decorating her otherwise impenetrable features. "I like things potent," she responded.

Jack smiled, eyeing the confirmation of this—the seven-carat wedding ring on her left hand as it twinkled briefly on the doorsill before she disappeared inside.

Normally, Jack would have taken a moment to analyze his apparent good fortune. But his guard was down (he'd already finished a half-bottle of Barolo), so he went with it and followed her into the room, careful to attenuate anything that might pass as exuberance.

Once inside, Jack found Claudia standing near the credenza holding an expensive, hand-blown bottle of grappa. He was impressed by her choice. He never thought for a moment such a delicate decanter would soon be the instrument of a brutal murder.

"They only made two hundred of these," she said proudly. "The last is at a vineria on the Rio San Rocco."

"I'm honored," said Jack.

"Don't be. I hate drinking alone," she replied as she handed him a glass of the vintage Picolit.

Jack winced a little at seeing the generous portion. The shot glasses she chose were more like mini-tumblers, those of a grappa enthusiast, or someone ready to let the alcohol drive for the night. Jack happened to be the latter, so he took the glass with a smile. It was then when he finally noticed the new arrivals—the mirrors, the lamp, and the imposing armoire.

"When did these arrive?" he asked confused.

"With me. I had them redone," she informed matter-of-factly.

Jack examined the side of the armoire. "Exceptional job. I'm impressed."

"You should be," she said confidently and then she raised her glass for a toast. Jack obliged and they drank. He grimaced. The stuff went down like Drano.

She smiled, amused by his discomfort. "Are

you interested in antiques, Mr. Sands?"

Jack braved a second shot to wash down the first and numb his throat. "Immensely. They're my business," he finally responded.

"Really. Restoration?"

"Recovery. I'm a private insurance investigator. Authenticity, theft, fraud—that sort of thing."

"How fascinating for you," she said, feigning admiration. "Which do you prefer?"

"I like *theft*. Gives me something to find. What about you?"

Claudia thought for a moment.

"I don't know—theft and fraud are so common. For me, I'd have to say *authenticity*," she said, eyeing him pointedly, "probably because it's so rare these days."

Jack watched her a beat, fascinated by her. Then something clicked as he eyed the bed.

"Don't tell me you're the one who redid this canopy?"

"The very same. Do you like it?"

"Like it?" Jack beamed. "I love it. It makes the room. Each night, I'd stare up at it—"

"How tragic. Why weren't you staring at the one you were with?"

"Because they commit you for that. It's called a hallucination."

"You mean you were alone."

"Always," he said as if deserving some kind of merit badge for his answer. "This place means a lot to me. I'm very careful who I share it with. You can understand. You're here alone, aren't you?"

Claudia stiffened almost imperceptibly. "And why would you think that?"

"Your luggage. And the fact you let me stay." Jack nodded to the single suitcase resting at the foot of the bed.

Claudia realized she'd been given away.

"Well, I guess you've found me out, Mr. Sands. Yes, I did come here alone. Actually, I came here to think."

Jack smiled and started for the door to the terrace. "Well, one always thinks better watching the sunset."

He tried to open the glass doors, but they were stuck. The lock had jammed. He fiddled with the mechanism lamenting, "It only does this when it's shut from the inside. I thought they fixed it."

He continued to work on it. It finally clicked open. Jack motioned her outside to the terrace. As she accepted his invitation and elegantly slinked past him, Jack took the time to savor it. There was a bit of leopard in her gait.

He should have been afraid. But he wasn't. In time, he would learn to regret that.

AN HOUR LATER, the setting sun had turned the Grand Canal into an undulating river of gold. High above it, on the table behind the balustrades on Room 502's private terrace, the bottle of rare Picolit was half-empty. Jack and Claudia hovered above it, seated across from each other intoxicated, more from the unexpected primal attraction coursing between them than from the pomace brandy of the vintage grappa.

Having had a head start on her with the Barolo, Jack seemed a little drunk. Claudia wasn't far behind. She sucked sensuously on a cigarette and seemed comfortable in his presence. Her features were somewhat hidden by the tongue of sheer black lace dangling from her hat. Still, the sun's ebbing glow managed to reflect in her simmering blue eyes, eyes Jack found himself getting lost in.

"So—when do I get my turn?" he asked.

"At what?"

"Secrets. We've been here two hours and you know all about me. You know I come here a lot. You know I came here this time because I've decided to divorce my wife."

Claudia turned away, briefly eyeing the canal traffic below. "You've been doing all the talking."

"That's the point. I don't even know your name."

"It's Claudia."

"That's a start. You said you came here to think?"

"It's rude and unmannerly to pry." She bristled.

"It's an occupational hazard. Indulge me."

She took another hit of the view and the grappa before giving the answer she knew would floor him. "I hate my husband, Mr. Sands," she revealed. "I came here to decide whether or not I should leave him."

She was right. Jack was stunned by the coincidence.

"Christ, it must be the room," he said. "Is this a recent development? The hate, I mean."

"I suppose I loved him once. When he had time for love. Now he only has time for lust. Business and lust."

"What's his business?"

"Shipping. His name is Bellini."

"Carlo Bellini? Transitalia?" Jack asked hesitantly.

"Do you know of him?"

"Of course. Who doesn't? Biggest tanker fleet in the Adriatic. Rumor has it the Camorra tops his client list."

"Shouldn't spread rumors, Mr. Sands. Some people find it terminal."

Jack stared at her a beat. Carlo Bellini was one of the richest men in Italy. And one of the most dangerous. Jack wasn't an idiot. He knew Bellini's reputation, but he was trying to fathom if her warning was intended to threaten or protect him. He decided to change gears as he poured himself another shot.

"So who's the object of his lust? Not you, I take it?"

She smiled cynically.

"No, not me. Someone he met in Paris. A model or some such thing. I don't know much about her except that he threatens to include her in his will."

"I think you're lying, Mrs. Bellini."

"What?" she asked, somewhat startled.

"You said you came to decide. I think you *already* decided to leave him."

She weighed his explanation and seemed relieved by his insight. "Maybe you're right. It's just that Carlo is a very complicated man to leave."

Jack looked in her eyes firmly with an almost boyish sincerity. "Look, you're one of the most attractive women I've ever met. You deserve better. Don't settle for less."

"Are you volunteering, Mr. Sands?" she probed, staring back at him.

Jack paused a long time. He wanted nothing more than to pick her up in his arms, carry her back inside, and devour every inch of her on top of his favorite Venetian bed. Instead, he calmly wiped the side of his mouth with a napkin and rose to leave.

"Some other time maybe," he said. "I've got to get back to Padua—to my wife. To tell her what you already know."

Claudia's desire for him peaked right at that instant. It wasn't just physical anymore. It was a strange, erotic attraction to his integrity. Integrity she'd never known in her own marriage. An integrity she'd longed for. She suddenly found herself getting wet, needing to have him. But she held back, revealing nothing.

"I'm sad for her," she said. "You seem like the kind of man a woman would be desperate to keep."

Jack smiled somewhat remorsefully.

"My marks as a husband have been less than stellar. She'll be better off. Divorce seems drastic, but sometimes in life, you gotta get drastic—you gotta do anything to free yourself. Trust me—*leave* the son of a bitch."

Jack started to say good-bye. She grabbed his hand softly.

"Couldn't you stay a little longer?" she asked. "A couple of hours, perhaps?"

Jack wavered for an instant. This was the first time they had touched. The warmth of her hand beckoned. Aroused him. He found the strength to override it.

"I haven't been a lot of things to my wife," he admitted, "but I have been loyal. Two more hours here could change that." He leaned down and kissed her hand. "I'll be back in two days. Things will be different then. Maybe we can see each other?"

She eyed him with a subtle hint of melancholy, so subtle Jack didn't even pick up on it. "I'm afraid that really won't be possible," she said softly.

"You seem like a resourceful woman, Mrs. Bellini," Jack said confidently. "*Make it* possible." With that, Jack nodded good-bye and walked away.

Claudia watched him, tantalized until he left the terrace, and disappeared back into the room. Seconds later, she heard the unmistakable wooden thud of the front door to Room 502 shutting behind him.

Claudia turned resignedly toward the whisper of crimson on the horizon. It was all that remained of the sun's fading glow.

A few pigeons descended stealthily onto the chimneys above her. The winged interlopers looked down upon Room 502's terrace. Perhaps they sensed the violent death that would soon take place there.

Claudia didn't notice. Her mind was too far away.

Chapter II

An oarsman gently steered a small boat past a row of serene villas lining a Paduan canal. He looked upward, startled suddenly by a *statue* rocketing toward him.

He ducked out of its trajectory nearly falling out of his boat as the statue plunged into the canal. Fist raised and shaking it wildly, he swore angrily at the window of a villa where a woman was screaming inside completely oblivious to the oarsman's plight below.

Inside the villa, a vase smashed hard against the wall scattering its shattered fragments on the floor where Jack lay, face down, covering his head from the onslaught.

His wife, Kate, hovered above him. She must've been beautiful once. But now her face was contorted with rage as she eyed the fractured remnants of the ancient vase on the floor with her husband cowering among them. "Was that Greek or Roman, Jack?!"

"It was Greek," Jack answered as he glared

up at her gathering the fragments.

"Really?" Kate said. "See, I don't remember where they're from anymore—just how long you were gone to bring them back. Two months for the Greek. And this one ..." She grabbed a primitive terra cotta Urn.

Jack freaked. "Dammit, Kate! *Not* the Etruscan!"

He moved toward her. She taunted him, threatening to throw it out the window. Jack froze.

"Oh, God forbid the *Etruscan!*" she said as she glared at the side of it. "It's just faded paint slapped on some clay! These people couldn't even *draw* for chrissakes! Why didn't you love me like you loved these *pots*?!"

She threw the vase at him. Jack leapt into the air and caught it. He set it down relieved. Then he finally crossed over to her consolingly. "I did love you, Kate."

She started to calm, her eyes tearing. "Yeah, Jack? And what about now?"

Jack's mind walked an emotional tightrope between honesty and diplomacy. His heart chose the former.

"I still love you," he assured her. "Just in a different way."

The palm of her hand hit his cheek like a

sledgehammer.

"You learned everything about art, Jack, but nothing about women. Women don't want the bullshit. They just want the truth. And the truth is you're still a little kid—always lookin' over the fence to see if maybe the grass is greener. Well, go ahead—jump over it—don't let me stop you."

Sometimes, the truth cuts like a knife. Jack tried to stop the bleeding with the rationalization he'd been relying on for months.

"Look we tried, all right," he said defensively. "Ten years, Kate! You hated Boston so we tried London. You hated London, we tried Paris …"

"It wasn't the cities, Jack. It was *you*. The fact you weren't there."

Jack bristled. "You knew about my work when you married me!"

"No, no, no, Mr. Memory Lapse. When I married you, you were a cop. At least you were home weekends."

"Don't start with that, Kate!" he yelled. "You know goddamn well why I quit!"

Jack hated revisiting those darker days, even via the protective conveyance of his memories. The two of them had barely survived. The scars were deep, and he had become an expert at disavowing them. But Kate still suffered from their memory. And now that she'd chosen to revisit them in her rage, she started to break, her hands batting away tears of remorse as she eyed Jack guiltily.

"I really loved you, Jack," she said, fighting not to weep.

Jack felt like shit. His mind was made up, but somehow, seeing her this frail, he found it hard to cope. A wave of guilt threatened to drown him. He held her in his arms fighting not to break himself. He was inching toward her, reconsidering when she pulled away abruptly wiping her eyes.

"Oh, fuck this maudlin crap. I'm relieved," Kate announced suddenly.

Jack was half-offended but half-relieved himself. "Yeah?" he prodded.

"It's been over for years," she answered. "I just couldn't face it." She started pacing, her anger and frustration ramping, regaining control. "I'm sick and tired of following you all over the planet, Jack. I used to think you'd stop," she said, pointing to the paintings, "figure out all this crap—"

"It's not crap, Kate," he said defensively. "It's *art!* It's ... it's *perfection!*"

"Perfection?!" she fired back. "On the outside, maybe, but on the inside, it's just canvas. It's not *real!*" Kate pointed to her heart angrily. "*This* is real, Jack! And I'm not like you. I don't need all the intrigue, the mystery, and the magic to jump start me in the morning." She poked an accusatory finger at him declaring, "Face it, Jack. You're *lost*."

The words resonated inside him. The truth always does. A feeble, "*Everybody's* lost, Kate," was the only defense he could muster.

"Yeah, well, not me," she said, turning away from him dismissively. "Go on, Jack. Get the hell out. Go back to Venice, to the alleys, to those frickin' grungy canals. What is it you always tell me? 'Venice is the only place in the world where time's stopped for three hundred years'…"

"Four hundred," Jack corrected.

"Yeah?? Well, you see that's where we're different—I *like* time. When it stops, I get nervous." She eyed him firmly, defiantly. "Good-bye, Jack."

There was a long, awkward moment between them. Jack finally moved toward her guiltily.

She blocked him with her hand. "*No*. Leave goddammit! Don't make it worse!"

He tried one more time to move toward her.

She wouldn't have it. Jack finally nodded. Then he turned and left.

She stood there a moment. Wondered if she should go after him. But he was already down the stairs. She shuddered, hearing him slam the door to the entrance two stories below. She started to break again, but she stopped herself. The anger took hold as she grabbed the Etruscan vase. She considered what she was about to do for about a millisecond. With the millisecond up, she jettisoned the vase out the window, and she marveled at how well two-thousand-year-old clay could fly.

On the Paduan canal below, the same Italian oarsman almost got nailed again on his return trip as the vase splashed into the water alongside him. Once again, voice shrill and fist raised, he railed at her angrily in Italian.

Kate glared down at him as she roared back, "Ahhh, Pasta Fungole Fettuccini Alfredo to you, pal!!" she screamed. Then she slammed the shutters exasperated yelling, "Christ, why doesn't anybody speak English around here!"

Her rage spent, Kate forced herself to calm. She eyed the shattered fragments of antiquity on her floor. They were a stark metaphor for her broken marriage. She thought of Jack, how she shut him down, how she closed off every possibility of a reprieve. She never thought for a moment the next time she saw him he'd probably be dead.

Chapter III

A high-speed commuter train snaked down serpentine tracks toward Venice.

Inside the first car, Jack stared at the ancient city approaching in the distance. As the train barreled across the Lagoon, his eyes walked an emotional tightrope between sadness and anticipation.

For years, his wife Kate, soon to be ex-wife, had been bedrock to an otherwise quixotic existence. She had grounded him, sometimes to the point of suffocation. He relied on her love's permanence, but the guilt he carried for his lack of reciprocity had begun to overwhelm him, more than the fear of life without her, the fear of life alone. Though Kate apparently knew the split was imminent, it still pained him to see her in such a fragile condition. His only solace was the fact he had never cheated on her, a fact she'd never believe, but a fact just the same. Somehow, his ten years of fidelity erased the guilt that might otherwise burden a man so eagerly anticipating a reunion with a possible new lover—a woman struggling to disentangle from a stale narrative of her own, a woman like *Claudia*.

Jack turned abruptly as a very old but well-dressed Italian man slid open the door to Jack's compartment and sat down in the empty seat across from him.

The man held a foil-wrapped bottle of wine and a box of Paduan chocolates laced tightly with a red ribbon. The man noticed Jack eyeing his delicately wrapped gifts and smiled politely.

Jack smiled back. His eyes drifted downward to the wrapped bottle on the old man's lap. It triggered the memory of another bottle. A bottle that would change his life forever. But to know this, Jack needed to see the future. Right now, all Jack could do with the future was to imagine it. And he imagined one in the comfort of Claudia's arms.

THE TRAIN HAD ARRIVED in Venice's Santa Lucia station. The passengers had all disembarked, including Jack, who stood now a mile away in the vast, tourist-ridden expanse of the Piazza San Marco.

A 600-year-old testament to Venetian

ingenuity, the Piazza was built on a million wood pilings driven deep into the mud of the lagoon forming a foundation for the towering monuments of a city-state that, in centuries past, dominated world trade.

Pigeons landed on the balustrades of the Doges Palace above Jack while he stood beneath them talking with someone on the other end of his cellphone.

"Buon giorno, Signor Rossini!" Jack said into his cell. "Yes, I'm back ... Thanks, yes, of course, I'll be staying with you ... Is Signora Bellini still at the hotel?"

Jack waited a beat and finally got the answer he had hoped for.

"She is? ... Excellent!" he said. "No, no. Don't ring her room. I want to surprise her."

Jack clicked off the call and removed a wrapped bottle of rare grappa from the bag he was holding. *Picolit 1985*. The bottle was identical to the one Claudia had served him from two days earlier. He eyed it expectantly then generously popped ten euros into the basket of a beggar who'd been silently soliciting on the stoop beneath him. Jack had a soft spot for beggars. He always donated generously thinking the practice might earn him some good luck. And good luck was high on his agenda this evening. Jack alerted to a gondolier's solicitation.

"Gondola, signor?" said an effusive, older gondolier approaching from the fondamenta.

"Sure. Why not?" Jack said as he smiled and followed the gondolier to his ebony gondola bobbing proudly on the lagoon.

"What's your name?" Jack asked as he climbed inside the gondola.

"Paolo, signor."

"Okay, Paolo. Take me to the Palazzo Giovanni."

"The scenic route, signor?" said the gondolier.

"You mean there's another one?" answered Jack smiling.

They both shared a laugh as Paolo leaned into his oar and the nose of the gondola started its habitual glide into the lagoon.

A FEW MINUTES LATER, Paolo's gondola swept around a corner into a small canal known as the Rio San Lucca. It slid past an elegant palazzo with the twelve signs of the zodiac etched into its side.

"We pass the house of Casanova, the master of amore!" said Paolo for perhaps the millionth time in his thirty-year career as a gondolier. Paolo eyed Jack's bottle and smiled. "And I see he might have a little competition this evening, eh, signor?

Jack smiled back, a bit embarrassed.

Paolo grinned. "She waits at Palazzo Giovanni?"

"Maybe," answered Jack as he eyed the restored remains of Casanova's old stomping grounds. A minor historian in his own right, Jack wondered what parts of the Casanova legend were really true. In his day, Casanova allegedly slept with 122 women. Pitiful, by today's standards (Fidel Castro boasted conquests in the thousands), yet for a city such as Venice, in such puritanical times, Casanova was a standout. The city's brooding nocturnal mystery lent itself to erotic fantasy. Fantasies Jack never indulged in. But tonight, Jack was hoping to change that.

Paolo's gondola slowed to navigate a corner that would finally reveal the magic of the Grand Canal beyond it. Jack watched as a motor boat roared by suddenly with blinking blue lights and its sirens blaring. It was followed by another motorboat with flashing red lights.

"What kind of boat was that, Paolo?" Jack asked.

"Carabinieri, signor. The police."

"Not the first one, Paolo. The last."

"That's the fireboat, signor," Paolo answered as he edged the gondola out into the Grand Canal where Jack watched the boats race to a nearby Palazzo and stop urgently beneath its terrace on the canal.

Jack's face filled with horror as he stared at the macabre, surreal image just three hundred yards in front of him.

The boats were circling *beneath the terrace* off Room 502 at the Palazzo Giovanni—the terrace where he had sat with Claudia—the terrace that was now host to a *BODY ON FIRE* on one of its chairs!

The fire blazed uncontrollably. Its flames knifed into the sky lighting up the canal. The fireboat's nozzle desperately sprayed gallons of water from the canal onto the carnage. Imagining the worst, Jack screamed at Paolo to get him to the Palazzo.

Chapter IV

The usually tranquil lobby of the Palazzo Giovanni was wrenching in chaos.

Screaming carabinieri, frantic firefighters, and an overwhelmed Rossini tried frantically to calm the guests who had run terrified from their rooms hearing the commotion.

Rossini spotted Jack as Jack pushed urgently through the crowd. Jack raced up the Giovanni's steps, three by three and arrived on the landing. He quickly moved through more firemen struggling past the hysterical chambermaid as he finally made his way into the open door of Room 502.

Jack barreled into the room almost knocking another carabiniere to the ground. He rushed out onto the terrace.

His face froze in disbelief as his worst fears were confirmed. Jack watched two firemen place the grotesque remains of *Claudia's charred body* on a stretcher. His heart bled seeing her burnt hat on the tile floor beside it.

A thickly accented Italian voice interrupted Jack's nightmare from behind.

"Did you know her, signor?" the man said calmly.

Jack turned finding Lucca Giovani, a middle-aged, fireplug of a man, a Captain of the Carabinieri, eyeing him warily.

"Yes. I knew her," Jack answered, struggling to speak and compose himself.

Lucca, sharp as a fox, stared at Jack's bottle with his coal brown eyes.

"May I see it?" Lucca asked, nodding to the bottle of grappa in Jack's hand.

"Huh?" Jack responded, confused and still reeling from the scene surrounding him.

"The bottle," Lucca clarified as he pointed at it.

Jack was still in a daze. He handed Lucca the bottle watching the stretcher as they carried Claudia's remains past him on the terrace. He fought his urge to vomit and turned back to Lucca.

"How did it happen?" Jack asked, still not believing that it had.

"This," answered Lucca holding up Jack's bottle of grappa. "She was drinking from a similar one on the terrace—the pills took effect—the bottle must have fallen on her and the cigarette she was smoking unwittingly set her on fire."

"Pills? What pills?" Jack asked confused.

Lucca turned to his assistant who was placing a bottle of prescription drugs into a plastic bag.

"*Seconal*. Signora Bellini committed suicide," Lucca said ominously. "She was probably already dead before the flames consumed her."

Jack collapsed into a chair. Lucca watched him carefully.

"How well did you know her, Mr. ...?

Jack was in shock. His answers were barely audible.

"Sands ... Jack Sands. I met her two days ago in this room. She was checking in, I was checking out."

"Did you sleep with her, Mr. Sands?"

"Absolutely not," Jack fired back irritated. "Why the hell would you ask me that?"

"The grappa," answered Lucca. "It's the same. Rare and expensive. You look like a man returning to his lover with gifts. I just assumed ..."

"Well, *don't* assume. We met. I told her I'd look her up when I got back. She was married, I never touched her."

"Unhappily married, according to this," Lucca said as he held up a letter written on fine Venetian stationary. "She left this suicide note on the pillow. Want to know what it says?"

Jack nodded and Lucca began reading.

My Dear Carlo...

Lucca looked up at Jack, "That was her husband."

"I know," Jack responded impatiently. "Keep reading."

Lucca refocused on the suicide note and continued reading Claudia's last words aloud.

I have given you ten years of my life and you have rewarded me with indifference and infidelity. My heart isn't capable of enduring any more torture. I met someone yesterday who helped me see things in a new light. Sometimes you must do something 'drastic' in order to be free...

The words cut Jack's heart like a knife. He was devastated by guilt. He felt responsible for pushing her over the edge. Lucca watched Jack's reaction carefully as he kept reading.

... I am taking my life so that I may find this freedom. May the guilt this causes you haunt you to your grave. And should your whore Franchesca find out about this note, I want the predatory bitch to know that she's nothing special. My dear husband Carlo has many whores, each unaware of the others. And may you all burn in hell—Claudia.

Lucca set down the note, eyeing Jack. "You made quite an impression on her."

"What's that supposed to mean?" Jack said, rising.

"Was she referring to you in the letter?" Lucca asked as he probed Jack's eyes for any sign of deceit.

"What if she was?" Jack answered defiantly. "Look, if you're trying to pin any blame on me ..."

"Please calm down, Mr. Sands. I merely said you made an impression," Lucca cautioned. Lucca had Jack right where he wanted him, on the defensive, on edge.

Jack turned irritated as *Rizzo,* a thin, weasel-faced carabiniere, bumped into him while gathering evidence. Rizzo glared at Jack then turned to Lucca mumbling something in Italian.

Lucca turned to Jack, "Unfortunately, I must ask you to leave. My men need room to work."

Jack suddenly snapped out of his confusion and finally realized where he was. He was a private investigator, an ex-cop, for god's sake. He quickly scanned the room looking for anything out of the ordinary. And, just as quickly, he found it.

The inside *knob* on the door leading from the room out onto the terrace, the one he had trouble opening two days earlier, the knob that was now *missing*. It was broken off.

"What happened to the door?" Jack asked Lucca.

"It was stuck. We had to break it to get out onto the terrace," Lucca answered dismissively. Then he motioned Jack outside. "If you'd be so kind, Mr. Sands."

His mind racing, Jack stared at the door for a few seconds then scanned the rest of the room carefully before he finally started to walk out.

Lucca called out after him, "I may have more questions. Where can I reach you?"

Jack had to formulate his plans on the spot, as his mind hadn't taken the time to go there. "I guess here at the hotel," he finally answered.

Lucca nodded and continued about his business. Jack left begrudgingly. He was devastated and distraught, but he was more consumed by the thought that he wasn't just leaving a room where a terrible tragedy had occurred. Jack had the overwhelming conviction that he was leaving a crime scene.

LATER THAT NIGHT, Jack slumped against a wall in Room 504, the room adjacent to 502. He was halfway through the bottle of grappa he had bought to share with Claudia. Her share would probably be the only thing that would help him sleep that night, the nail in the coffin of his drunken stupor.

Jack looked like shit. He dialed a number on his cellphone. After a few seconds, he heard a recording of Kate's voice on the other end.

"Hi, you've reached Kate Nelligan ..." Kate's cheerful voice announced crisply.

Christ, she's already using her maiden name, Jack thought to himself as Kate's lengthy recording continued...

"I've gone back to New York so please leave a message after the tone. Jack, if it's you— I don't want you calling me. And Jack..."

Jack perked, hoping for some kindness to soothe his misery.

"*I threw out the Etruscan.*"

Click. Dial tone.

"*Bitch!*" Jack grumbled as he downed another shot of grappa in anger. He stopped midway from downing another as he caught sight of *flashlights* dancing outside on the terrace off Room 502.

Jack crawled over to the window. He checked his watch. Three a.m. He clicked off the lights in the room and strained to clarify the *shadows* weaving amongst the shards of light outside on the terrace.

He managed to make out four men amongst the terrace's maze of statues and topiary in the moonlight. The beams of their flashlights were crisscrossing the balustrades where Claudia's suicide took place.

Jack opened the window. As the men became illuminated under the moonlight, he saw they were not the police. He tried to listen to what they were saying but could only hear whispers interspersed with faint sounds from the sleepy canal below. As the men started to leave, Jack got up and headed to the door of his room.

He quickly went outside into the portego

and crossed to the half-open door of Room 502.

Inside 502, Jack found a thin man in a dark suit on his knees searching for something under the bed. Vitale Donato turned, alarmed, finding Jack staring at him. Mid-fiftyish and arrogant, Donato was somewhat sinister looking. Jack eyed him suspiciously.

"Lose something?" Jack asked bluntly.

Donato was startled but recovered quickly with a thin smile. "Yes," he responded as he bent back down and came up with a gold pen. From Jack's angle, he couldn't really tell if Donato found it or if he was just covering his tracks with it.

Before Jack could pursue it further, Rossini, the hotel manager, walked in from the terrace with three other men. The first, Antonio Torelli, a short, sixtyish, fireplug of a man, eyed Donato oddly witnessing Jack's intrusion. Behind Torelli was Carlo Bellini, fifty-six, impassive and imposing. Carlo was flanked by a bodyguard built like a skyscraper.

"My apologies, Mr. Sands," said Rossini, breaking the awkward silence. "I hope we didn't disturb you?"

"I was having trouble sleeping," Jack said, sizing up the shady trio in front of him. "I thought I'd go for a walk."

"Under the circumstances, who can blame you?" Rossini sympathized. "It's been tragic. So very, very tragic."

The other men would have been happy to let Jack leave unintroduced, but Jack pushed it by lingering. Rossini finally caved.

"Mr. Sands, allow me to introduce Signors Donato, Torelli, and Bellini," said Rossini. "Signor Bellini was the husband of ..."

"I know who you are," Jack said as he extended a hand to Bellini, forcing a sympathetic smile. "I'm so sorry. You must be in shock."

Bellini shook Jack's hand reticently. He seemed anything but distraught.

Rossini tried clumsily to ease the awkwardness. "Mr. Sands met Claudia only two days earlier," Rossini offered, immediately wishing that he hadn't.

Bellini glared at Jack.

"We met only briefly," Jack said as he stared back at Bellini brazenly. "I liked her. Can't imagine why someone would cheat on her."

Bellini eyed Jack menacingly. Then he brushed past him. Torelli and Donato followed, each offended by Jack's remarks. Jack wouldn't let it lay as they filed out.

"Was Franchesca worth it, Carlo?" Jack called out bitterly.

Bellini spun in his tracks. His bodyguard walked forcefully over to Jack as Torelli grimaced like a Pit Bull. Bellini called both of them off with his eyes. Then he walked up calmly to Jack.

"In Venice, we value respect more than our tourists," said Bellini as he got within inches of Jack's face.

"I'm not a tourist, Bellini," replied Jack standing his ground.

Bellini stared at Jack a moment then offered him a thin smile.

"A pity," said Bellini. "Tourism is the only thing that survives in Venice. Everything else just *decays* and gets swallowed up by the lagoon. Ciao, Mr. Sands."

Bellini nodded a curt goodbye and Jack watched Carlo and his entourage head out the door. After they had disappeared into the portego, Jack eyed the floor where Torelli was searching for an instant before Rossini managed to press him out of the room.

Chapter V

Decaying oil and faded pigment was all that remained of the epic painting of a man slitting the throat of another. It was now in its rightful place on the eastern wall inside the Accademia, one of Venice's largest museums. Jack stood alongside it next to Giorgio Sanudo, the museum's dapper, middle-aged curator, as Giorgio inspected the five-hundred-year-old masterpiece.

"Only a Venetian could make murder so beautiful," marveled Giorgio as he admired the work. "It's nice to have Cain and Abel back in the family."

"Cairo's the last place I thought I'd track down a stolen Tintoretto," Jack allowed, "but, what the hell, fratricide's always big at a Sheik's auction."

Giorgio smiled as they walked down a corridor lined with Venetian masterpieces. Jack and Giorgio had been friends for over a decade. Giorgio first spotted the transplanted, out of work cop from Boston on one of his weekly visits to the museums of Venice. Jack was the grandson of an American Army Colonel tasked with retrieving stolen art from the Nazis at the end of World War II. He grew up listening to stories of finding lost treasure on his grandfather's lap. By the age of twelve, he discovered what the word *art* really meant as he accompanied his grandfather to various museums exhibiting the famous paintings his grandfather had recovered. The paintings were interesting, but the stories surrounding their retrieval interested Jack more. They held sway with his imagination. Jack always fancied a life like his grandfather and, later in his own, he finally obtained it. Giorgio valued Jack's passion as a connoisseur, but he valued Jack's lethality as an ex-cop even more. He studied Jack as they headed down another corridor.

"I still don't understand how you managed to retrieve the painting."

"Simple. I was the highest bidder," Jack revealed. "I paid him with the forgery they substituted for your original when they stole it from your warehouse."

"And he accepted without a fight?" Giorgio asked with a raised and skeptical brow.

"Not exactly," Jack said. "But a certain

malleability set in when he watched me persuade his two bodyguards that their lives would be richer without a bullet in their foreheads."

"Sounds like a reasonable argument," Giorgio grinned.

"Well, it certainly helped *reason* prevail. Let's face it, Giorgio, he can still exhibit the forgery on his bedroom wall. And if any woman he's bedding has enough time on her hands to spot the fake, he's got bigger problems than a soft canvas."

The two shared a laugh as they finally reached Giorgio's office.

Jack hovered above Giorgio's desk while Giorgio took a seat behind it. Giorgio pulled out a corporate checkbook from a drawer and wrote a check for Jack's services.

"I've often wondered what would become of you, Jack, if people ever stopped stealing art," Giorgio said, handing Jack the check.

"They'll never stop, Giorgio. The stuff's too seductive," Jack said, pocketing his earnings. "A masterpiece only comes along once a century, like the perfect woman. What do you know about Claudia Bellini?"

Giorgio was thrown for a second but quickly figured out where Jack's question was leading.

"I heard you met her at the Giovanni?"

"Word travels fast," Jack said.

"The canals are small, the echoes large," Giorgio said with a thin smile. "Especially when they echo the name *Bellini*. I worked at his law firm before coming to the museum." Giorgio eyed Jack pointedly. "Stay out if it, Jack. Bellini likes his image pristine. He'll act decisively to contain the scandal."

"Bellini impress you as a violent man, Giorgio?"

"He's a lamb compared to his two partners, Donato and Torelli," Giorgio cautioned.

Jack smiled. "They're a real chummy trio. We rubbed shoulders at the Palazzo."

"In business, the three of them are lethal. They built Transitalia from nothing."

"With a little help from La Cosa Nostra and the Camorra," Jack reminded.

"That's never been proven," answered Giorgio as he shifted uncomfortably in his chair. "Nonetheless, Claudia threatened to tear the company apart."

"How's that?" Jack pressed.

Giorgio hesitated before answering. But it was his own fault that Jack's curiosity had been awakened. And Giorgio knew, more than anyone else, how once awakened, this curiosity would never sleep. So Giorgio reluctantly explained.

"Three months ago, a large Benelux concern offered three billion dollars to buy the company. Claudia was pressing Carlo to sell."

"So why didn't he?" Jack asked confused. "Three billion is a lot of cash."

"I'm afraid not nearly enough to buy Venetian pride. The partners are adamant Transitalia remain Venetian."

"So poor Claudia didn't have a chance?"

"Claudia was a bitch, Jack," Giorgio said firmly. "She fought with Carlo in public and embarrassed his partners at every opportunity."

"Even a bitch doesn't deserve to die like she did," Jack interrupted bitterly.

"People commit suicide of their own free will, Jack."

"I'm not talking about suicide, Giorgio," Jack said sharply. "I'm talking about *murder*.

BLUE AND RED carabinieri uniforms crisscrossed police headquarters as Jack argued heatedly with Lucca inside his office on the Riva degli Schiavoni.

"... because I know the room, Lucca! The door had to be shut from the inside for it to jam," Jack insisted. "Someone else was in there the night of the murder."

"Suicide, Mr. Sands," Lucca said firmly. "*Suicide.*"

"Call it what you want," Jack said frustrated. "Did your lab check the note for authenticity?"

"Of course. It was definitely Claudia Bellini's handwriting."

"Then it was written under duress. And what about the grappa? A body doesn't burn like that from a shot of grappa!"

"Her dress was made from Istrian silk. It's extremely flammable," Lucca explained, his patience wearing thin. "The matter is *closed,* Mr. Sands."

"Look, I was with her for hours. The woman *was not* suicidal!"

Lucca prided himself on his diplomacy. It had served him well in his three-decade tenure in the Veneto, but Jack's intractability was exhausting. Lucca stood up and eyed Jack irritated.

"I suggest maybe you need a break from Venice. It's Carnival time and the crowds can be oppressive."

"The crowds or Carlo Bellini?"

Jack was sharp. Lucca gave him that much. But Carlo Bellini was a force to reckon with, especially in Venice, a place where a superior's loyalty can evaporate at a moment's inconvenience. Lucca eyed Jack firmly.

"Bellini's already filed a harassment complaint against you. If you insist on further allegations, I cannot be responsible for his actions."

Lucca moved past Jack dismissively. "Ciao, Mr. Sands." He exited into the corridor leaving Jack hanging there frustrated and alone.

Chapter VI

A motoscafo dropped off Jack at the Palazzo Giovanni's side landing.

From across the square, someone in a carnival costume watched him from the shadows. It was the *assassin* from the opening sequence. The Assassin watched with interest as Jack headed into the front doors of the hotel.

Moments later, Jack was at the Giovanni's lobby desk in front of Rossini. Rossini was nervous. He was obviously the current recipient of Jack's incessant prodding.

"It's a rather unusual request under the circumstances. The room hasn't been properly cleaned," Rossini said feebly.

"C'mon, Rossini," Jack pleaded. "502 is my favorite room, and it's no good to anybody vacant. The sooner someone *stays* in it, the sooner things will get back to normal."

Rossini finally acquiesced, his pliability no doubt motivated by the hundred euro note Jack slipped into his hand. Rossini grabbed the key to Room 502 and gave it to Jack. Jack winked gratefully.

"Thanks, Rossini. You did the right thing."

Jack turned and headed up the stairway. Rossini regretted his compliance by the time Jack disappeared onto the upper portego.

AN HOUR HAD PASSED, but Jack hadn't noticed. He was too busy tearing apart the furniture inside Room 502 looking for evidence.

With an almost trance-like fury—

Jack searched the floor where Torelli had been searching the night before.

He lifted the mattress and searched every crevice beneath it.

He rolled up the rug searching every inch of the baroque marble floor.

He took each picture off the wall searching behind them, revealing their darkened silhouettes on the wallpaper they vacated.

He inspected the ornate, crossed-sword coat of arms hanging by the front door.

Jack finally backed away frustrated. His search had yielded nothing but a dusty and disheveled room.

He collapsed on the bed downing a healthy shot of grappa. He played the first night he met Claudia over and over again in his mind. He visualized every footstep he took that night, even every step he *didn't* take, which made him suddenly beeline to the bathroom.

TEN MINUTES LATER, Jack was on his hands and knees inspecting the marble floor of the bathroom in Room 502. God knows how many nights the Giovanni's guests had spent there in a similar position, hovering over the toilet after a night of binge-filled serial partying at the Carnival's decadent venues.

It was getting dark and the subtle lighting of the bathroom wasn't anywhere near bright enough, so Jack struck a match to look behind the bidet.

Unfortunately, like the hour-long endeavor that preceded this, Jack came up empty. He stared defeated in the mirror as the match continued to burn unchecked between his fingers.

Jack winced when the flame reached his fingertips and he tossed it into the tub.

WHOOSH! The drain lit up and spit out an angry, bluish flame.

Jack lunged for a towel and tossed it on top of the drain. He stared at the smoldering terry cloth bewildered for a moment—until it hit him.

Jack's face suddenly brightened. He pulled

back the towel from the extinguished flames. Then, curiously, he *stuck his finger* in the drain.

He pulled it out and examined a weird, gooey liquid on the end of it. He tasted it cautiously. His eyes lit up.

Jack spun around and raced back inside the main room. He grabbed the bottle of grappa on the table, poured a touch into the shot glass, and dipped a second finger into it. He tasted it. Then he took another taste of the finger he pulled out of the drain.

"Son of a bitch..." Jack said out loud, his thoughts ratcheting to warp speed realizing the two liquids tasted *exactly the same.*

Jack quickly reached over and took a saucer from beneath a cup of espresso. He rubbed the liquid from the drain onto one-half of the saucer and poured a dab of fresh grappa from the bottle on the other half.

He struck a match and lit them both. He stood back and watched as *they burned exactly the same color.*

Jack was on a roll. He thought a moment. Something clicked. He raced over to the closet and grabbed a wire coat hanger. He unraveled it as he headed back into the bathroom.

In seconds, he was hovering over the tub

again. This time, he was snaking the wire down the drain like a neurosurgeon. He fiddled with it hearing something rattling inside. He fought with it frustrated until he finally *hooked something substantial*. He smiled as he pulled up his catch, eyeing a gunk-coated, *metallic form* on the end of the wire.

He quickly wiped the gunk and ooze from the tiny metal object and stared in awe at the treasure he had retrieved—*a large silver ring* embellished with a *winged lion and a serpent*.

Jack held it up to the light and inspected it when, suddenly, a *loud knock* on the front door startled him.

Jack was rattled. The room was a mess. He quickly placed the ring in a tissue and slipped it into his pocket as the knocking resumed.

He shoved the coat hanger under the rug. He started to straighten up the place. In doing so, he unwittingly banged his head on the bedpost as the knocking got louder.

"Just a minute!" Jack yelled irritated.

Pissed, he threw on a shirt and finally opened the door. His features softened when he found himself staring at an *almond-eyed, dark-haired, tanned bombshell* standing outside in the portego.

"Sorry for barging in on you like this," said

the woman, shifting her weight awkwardly. "I'm a reporter. Actually, strike that. Technically, I'm a tourist on vacation. I was leaving for Florence tonight when my editor calls all frantic telling me to stay and cover this suicide thing…"

Jack was mesmerized by her beauty for a nanosecond, but it wore off quickly when he realized the predatory nature of her intrusion.

"I've got nothing to say," he told her irritated. "Talk to the carabinieri." He started to close the door on her.

She jammed her foot in it and glared back at him. "Look, it took me over *an hour* to get here! The vaporettos were jammed," she said, shifting her weight again. "The least you can do is let me use your bathroom. The one in the lobby is out of order."

Jack was reluctant, but she was moving about as if something inside her was about to burst. He looked back scanning the room for any obvious sign of what he'd been doing only moments before. He finally nodded and motioned her inside.

"It's the door on the right," Jack said as she blew past him and made a beeline for it.

"Jesus, what happened to this place?" she said, eyeing the unkempt chaos that Jack hadn't managed to hide.

Jack watched the bathroom door shut behind her without answering. Then he feverishly straightened up the room, talking on the move.

"I didn't get your name?" Jack called out.

"Amanda Parks. What's yours?" she yelled from inside the bathroom.

"Jack Sands," he said, making up the bed.

"Oh, right—the insurance investigator who was with her before she did it. Was she a nutcase or what?"

"How did you know I knew her?" he said, thrown, as he shoved the saucer and spoon into his luggage.

Amanda emerged from the bathroom and caught him at it. "Short on dinnerware, Jack?"

Jack looked up embarrassed.

"Don't worry, I won't tell. With me it's towels," she said smiling as she studied the room. "I read it in Il Gazzettino."

"Read what?" Jack asked confused.

"The story. You asked how I knew, remember? You were the last to see her alive."

"Word travels fast," Jack muttered surprised.

"The canals are small, the echoes large."

"Where'd you get that line?" he asked, remembering he had heard it from Giorgio earlier in the day.

"Out of a book. Snappy line, isn't it? I like snappy lines—I'm a writer."

"For who?"

"Gossip rag in upstate New York—the Syracuse Herald." Amanda studied the gilded bed. "Wow. This thing's incredible!" She turned back to him and started to unbutton her jacket. "Mind if I take off my coat? I'm burning up in here."

"Some other time," Jack said, becoming increasingly rattled by her presence. "Look, Miss Parks, this whole ordeal has been very distressing for me, so—"

"—I can imagine. It must have come as one helluva shock. Was she pretty?"

"She was beautiful."

Amanda sensed his sadness and put a tender, seemingly genuine, hand on his shoulder.

"She really got to you, didn't she? Why do you think she killed herself?"

Jack snapped out of his momentary melancholy and wiped her hand off his shoulder. He headed to the door agitated, motioning her to follow.

"For the record, Miss Parks, I don't think she killed herself, and if you don't mind, I'd like a little privacy."

Amanda perked hearing his words. "You mean you think someone *killed* her?"

Jack didn't respond. He just started nudging her out the door.

"You have evidence?" she pressed. "C'mon, Jack. I'm American, for God's sake. We have to stick together."

He finally managed to squeeze her back out the door. He eyed her dismissively. "Nice meeting you, Miss Parks. Enjoy Florence."

Jack shut the door behind her and leaned against it. He waited a moment and then sighed relieved at the absence of any more knocking.

Outside in the portego, Amanda stared at the closed door, pissed, a few moments before finally moving sullenly toward the stairs.

As she passed, the chambermaid watched her from the shadow of a doorway. And for some reason, the chambermaid smiled.

Chapter VII

Early the next morning, Jack stood next to Giorgio, both of them staring at the ring Jack had found in the tub. It was now resting on a glass slide in a lab while a technician examined it under a microscope.

"It's authentic Fortuny," the technician said reverentially. "Only five were made. Unfortunately, this one is absent any fingerprints or DNA."

"Probably burnt off by the fire in the drain," Jack surmised. "What about the fluid analysis?"

The lab technician moved to a petri dish that presumably contained the remains of the gooey liquid Jack found in Room 502's drain.

"You were correct. It was definitely grappa. And it was the same as in the other bottle—Picolit 1985," the tech answered. "A pity someone felt the need to waste it."

Jack smiled vindicated at Giorgio. Giorgio nodded and began his reluctant morph from skeptic to believer.

MOMENTS LATER, on the spiral staircase winding through floor after floor of baroque art hanging in the Accademia, Jack was in full bloom as he pieced it all together. Giorgio envied Jack's reverse engineering skills when it came to crime solving. Giorgio was a master at spotting forgeries, and he knew Jack was the real thing. He grew impatient with Jack's silence.

"*So*? What's your theory?" Giorgio asked Jack, assuming he not only had one, but that it would be bulletproof.

"The killer had to make sure she'd burn."

"Why?"

"Because he probably beat her and shoved her around. The bruised flesh would've tipped the coroner that the suicide was a phony. I say he knocked her out, stuffed her in the tub, and then emptied the grappa on her to make sure she was flammable."

"And what about the ring?" Giorgio pressed, confident that Jack's logic was impeccable so far.

"It must've slipped off the killer's hand in the commotion and clogged the drain. The excess grappa collected on top of it."

Giorgio's skepticism resurfaced. "Then why didn't someone see him drag the body onto the terrace?'

"You can only see the terrace from Room 502 and 504. Room 504 was empty that day, I checked," Jack said confidently. "There's no other explanation, Giorgio. That grappa's worth 500 euros a bottle. It's *not* the kind of thing you pour into a tub."

While Giorgio wasn't entirely convinced, he was certain Jack's theories were worth pursuing. Also, if Jack was correct, his findings were certain to ignite a juicy Venetian scandal, the kind Giorgio liked having his finger in.

It was good for business, a real icebreaker at an exhibition. Venice's elite rarely got their hands dirty except when foraging through the latest gossip.

"We'll call the carabinieri," Giorgio said with authority.

"No. It's evidence, but it's not conclusive. If I give this to Lucca now, he'll bury it. Especially if it leads to Bellini."

"So what then? You'll just sit on this? That's not like you, Jack."

"Who said anything about sitting?" Jack answered. "When I find out the ring's pedigree, I'll find the killer. I'll be in touch." Jack nodded good-bye and quickly headed out the main doors of the Accademia.

IN A SMALL CALLE devoid of tourists off the Grand Canal, Jack slipped out of a tiny antique shop, one of the seven he'd been to in the last three hours. He placed the ring back in his pocket, having no luck finding out anything about either its pedigree or its identity.

The Fortuny was so rare most Venetian merchants weren't even aware of its existence, or, if they were, they were skeptical that Jack possessed the real thing. Jack eyed a list in his hand. It itemized the remaining shops in Venice that might have some knowledge of the ring.

As the sun beat down upon him, its glare prevented him from noticing a short, leather-faced man watching him from behind a column. Choosing the next antique shop on the list, Jack headed toward another calle across the square. The short man followed.

TEN MINUTES LATER, Jack walked down yet another narrow calle. Gondolas drifted by, and the inevitable spectator pigeons looked on, perching on seventeenth century balconies. Jack stopped in his tracks hearing a *woman yelling* in the lobby of a small hotel. The woman's voice was familiar.

"*Non Libere! Non Libere!* That's all I hear from you people! Put a sign out front to tip us off!" Amanda was screaming from inside the lobby as the hotel desk clerk yelled back at her in Italian.

Jack watched as Amanda returned fire, in broken Italian for sure, but with gestures that were full-blown Neapolitan.

They made the clerk cringe as Amanda jerked her suitcases off the floor and stomped out of the hotel lobby onto the narrow calle. Jack shook his head, smiling. He set out after her, finally catching up to her at the edge of a large campo.

"How about you let me carry that for you?" Jack offered, reaching for one of her bags.

Amanda turned. Saw him. Frowned. Then kept walking. "How about you jump into a canal and make like a blowfish," she snapped without turning.

Jack liked her spunk. He grabbed her bag.

"Look, let me help you. You caught me at a bad time."

"Yeah, pal?? Well, you caught me at a bad time, too! I got blisters on my feet the size of walnuts. Carnival time, capisce?" she said glaring at him. "Non libere! No more decent rooms in Venice! Last night I had to stay in a youth hostel!"

"What happened to Florence?"

"My editor, inconsiderate prick that he is, wants me *here*. I told him it's useless because the carabinieri won't comment, and the *one guy* who might, threw me out of his room with the trash."

"I had my reasons," Jack said guiltily.

"That's no excuse. I was just doing my job. Can't you understand that?"

Jack felt like a schmuck. She looked beat. Her fingers were blistered from toting around her luggage like a gypsy. He eyed her genuinely.

"Look, let me make it up to you. Start with a cup of coffee?"

Amanda began to soften. She eyed a high fashion boutique behind them and pointed to its window. "How about starting with that linen suit? Really show me you care."

"Let's work up to the suit. Okay? Start with coffee?"

Jack smiled. Then Amanda finally smiled. And she was drop dead gorgeous when she smiled.

And from Jack's perspective, the perspective of a man who had just had his world turned upside down, this was just fine.

He grabbed her bags, which she allowed, and they headed off together toward the Piazza San Marco.

Chapter VIII

The pigeons amassing at the feet of the patrons of the Café Florian on the northern edge of the Piazza San Marco were especially active that day. The morning fog had lifted and the sunshine inspired an upbeat generosity from the Florian's clientele, at least in regards to breadcrumbs—which, if priced as a percentage of the Florian's normally egregious bar tabs, were expensive feed indeed. Amanda doled out her share from a basket of thin Venetian bread sticks as she watched Jack returning from the bar inside with two espressos served in the Florian's legendary fine China. He had to weave through a barrage of costumed but subdued carnival goers, who were mainlining caffeine to recover from their pre-dawn debauchery.

Jack finally arrived at their table but not before stopping to drop five euros into an old beggar's basket on the way. He sat down next to Amanda. She was busy batting away second-hand smoke from a fat patron dressed as a clown with a belly the size of the circus tent you'd typically find one performing in. She eyed the beggar that Jack donated to on the way over to her. "Fond of beggars, Jack?"

Jack smiled and sat down next to her, handing her the cup of espresso. "Yeah. Sometimes I think I'm looking in the mirror."

"Really? Does it scare you?"

"Only when they wink," Jack answered as he dug into his pocket fishing for something. "Dolcificante? Don't know why, but they never have any on the table here."

Amanda nodded as Jack pulled out a couple of packets of artificial sweetener. In the process, the *Fortuny ring* fell out of his pocket and dropped to the ground. It bounced once with a dull ping and came to rest near Amanda's left foot. She promptly retrieved it, admired it briefly, and finally handed it back to him. "What a gorgeous piece. Where'd you get it?" she asked.

Jack almost jerked it out of her hand.

"I was only looking," Amanda said offended.

"Sorry. It's just that—well, it's just that it's not mine."

"So whose is it?" she asked sensing his awkwardness.

"Truth?" he said. She nodded. "I really don't know." Jack turned toward the Lagoon anxious to change the subject. "The view from here is spectacular, don't you think?"

"Yeah—and how about those Mets?" Amanda answered irritated as she grabbed her suitcases and started to leave in a huff.

Jack jumped up to stop her. "Wait a minute! What's got into you?"

"I don't like being patronized, Jack! I'm not stupid. You're obsessed with this murder thing. It's eating away at you. If you want to keep it to yourself, fine, but you're making a big mistake. I'm a reporter. I'm *trained* for this. I can *help* you."

Then she just shook her head and walked away from the table.

Jack followed after her as she began chastising herself out loud. "Christ, why are we even having this conversation? I'm on my vacation, for God's sake! I came to Italy to have fun, to get crazy, to ..."

Jack finally caught up with her as she reached the center of the Piazzo San Marco. He spun her around. "Are you finished?"

"I haven't even warmed up," she fired back.

"Do they have ethics in upstate New

York?" Jack asked warily.

"Sure. You buy them by the set. Just like in Washington."

Jack looked into her eyes briefly, trying to size her up. Finally, he opened up. "If I let you in on this, can I trust you not to break the story until I get to the bottom of it?"

"Of course. *If* you promise me the exclusive." Unlike the mass of pigeons swarming at their feet, Amanda wasn't interested in breadcrumbs.

Jack considered it a moment. Physically, there was nothing about Amanda any man with a heartbeat wouldn't be mad for, but her tenacity and stubbornness was particularly attractive to him. It reminded him of himself. And he needed an ally that wasn't beholden to the Venetian elite. He trusted Giorgio implicitly, but Giorgio was born, bred, and would probably die in the Veneto. He needed help from someone on the outside, and he decided to take a chance on the fiery young reporter who was impatiently standing in front of him.

"Fair enough," Jack said, holding up the Fortuny ring. "I've got evidence that Claudia's killer may have worn this ring. It's one of five. If I find out who sold it, I may get a line on the guy's identity."

"That's easy," Amanda said confidently. "We'll hit the antique shops. I've spent my paycheck in half of them."

"I've been to ten. No one knows the merchandise."

Amanda eyed him curiously. "You're a driven man. How long were you in love with her?"

"*Love?* I never even touched her."

"That's the problem with men, Jack," she said as she picked up her bags again. "You think love has to start in the fingers."

Amanda headed off toward the Doges Palace, as Jack stood there confused. "*Now* where are you running to?"

"I'll catch up with you later," she yelled over her shoulder. "I gotta find a better room!"

With that, Jack watched her fade into a sea of Carnival costumes parading through the piazza.

LATER THAT NIGHT, a shopkeeper shrugged as Jack showed him the ring. Jack nodded thanks and exited yet another antique shop coming up dry for the fifteenth time in less than fifteen hours.

Jack was beat. It was dark. Though warm throughout the day, the fog had drifted back in, and with it, the winter chill of the Adriatic, which cut like a knife. Jack headed back toward the Giovanni, giving it up for the night.

He favored a shortcut that would take him through the fish market, not knowing his path would mirror the path of the woman who was murdered by the masked assassin a few days earlier.

The now deserted, column-rimmed fish market fronted the Grand Canal just moments from the Rialto by Gondola. But getting there on foot required a fifteen-minute walk through a tortured maze of narrow Venetian calles. In foggy conditions such as these, the route demanded a deft navigator.

The damp Venetian fog always amplified the sound of any and everything. Tonight, it was amplifying the sound of footsteps. Not Jack's—but the footsteps of the man tailing him.

Jack turned abruptly, spotting a *large man* thirty meters behind him. The large man ducked behind a column. Jack moved away, quickening his pace. He heard more footsteps behind him. Jack turned around rattled, looking to his left. Nothing. He spun to his right. There! Not the large man, but the *small man* who was tailing him a day earlier.

Jack slipped away, snaking down another narrow calle. He quickly looked behind him. Clear. He knifed down another calle just to make sure he'd lost the tail. Then he started to run as—

A *thick arm* cold cocked him from a doorway. Jack plunged to the ground. The large man he saw earlier pounced on him like a Doberman. He shoved Jack against a wall. The small man appeared and joined in on the beating.

They pummeled Jack's chest with sledgehammer blows. Jack couldn't breathe, let alone talk. They finally ran out of steam.

Jack slumped to the pavement. The large man jerked him back up by the collar and poked his coarse, menacing face into Jack's—

"This is so that you should know respect," he grunted icily.

With that, the large man viciously headbutted Jack. Jack slammed back down to the pavement unconscious.

Chapter IX

Three hours later, the fog dominated all of Venice, including the inside of Jack's head. He was spread out on the bed inside Room 502 with ice packs over his chest. Jack was bruised, pissed, and on his cellphone to Giorgio.

"... it was dark, Giorgio. The guy was big and ugly. Those are the only two adjectives I can come up with."

Giorgio was inside his apartment pacing past the few items of his minimalist modern décor. He looked briefly outside a porthole-shaped window at the Piazza San Marco below. Giorgio's view was as enviable as the collection of art crowding his walls. "You sure it wasn't the bodyguard you met with Bellini at the hotel?"

"No. Bellini's guy was a skyscraper," Jack said, shifting position uncomfortably on the bed. "This guy was just *big*."

"I warned you, Jack."

"Look, Giorgio, if I weren't getting warm,

they wouldn't have muscled me. I need your help!"

Giorgio slumped down apprehensively in the chair behind his desk. "I'm just a curator in a museum. What could I possibly..."

"You're an *ex-partner* in his law firm, practically family!" Jack pressed. "Claudia's funeral is tomorrow. Drop by and pay your respects. You might overhear something."

Giorgio picked up the newspaper lying on his desk and eyed a prominent headline proclaiming Claudia's suicide. "Bellini's our biggest patron, Jack. This really isn't the kind of thing I should get involved in."

Jack beat his knuckles against the mic hole of his cell phone, and then he spoke into it, agitated. "I think we have a bad line, Giorgio! I'm the guy who took a knife in the gut for you in Naples, a bullet in the hip in Florence!"

Giorgio squirmed uncomfortably in his chair. "Okay, okay. I'll go to the funeral."

Jack smiled to himself on the bed. But the smile quickly disappeared as he heard a *loud knock* on the door to Room 502.

"Thanks, Giorgio. Means a lot to me." Jack clicked off quickly hearing another knock. He looked around for some protection as Lucca had confiscated his gun for safekeeping after questioning him at Carabinieri headquarters. Jack finally grabbed a *dagger* from the coat of arms hanging on the wall near the door. He eased over to the door as the incessant knocking continued.

"Yes?!" he barked at the closed door irritated, firmly grasping the dagger.

A weird, artificially deep voice oozed through the door from the portego. "Message for Mr. Sands," barked the voice.

The voice rattled Jack. "A message from who?"

And the weird voice barked back, "Open the door or I'll break it down."

Pissed now, but staying cautious, Jack slid open the brass disc covering the peephole and stared out into the portego. The palm of a hand was covering his view from the outside. Jack was in no mood for bullshit. He firmly grasped the long dagger with one hand and the door latch with the other.

WHOOSH! Jack swung open the door. A body jumped in front of him. He grabbed the person and threw them to the floor. They recovered and struggled to stand. Jack was ready to pounce when he finally realized it was *Amanda.*

"Are you nuts?! What are you doing?!"

Amanda yelled angrily.

Jack's adrenaline was pumping hard. He slammed the door shut. "What am I doing? What are *you* doing! And what's with that ridiculous voice?" he fired back incredulous.

Amanda stood up and retrieved the *shopping bag* she was carrying from the floor.

"I was just having some fun, okay? I'm a little drunk. I'm sorry," she said teetering, trying to keep her balance. "Let me amend that statement, I'm *very* drunk. I've had a drink in every hotel that didn't have a vacancy." Amanda finally spotted the dagger. "Jesus, who are you? Jack the Ripper?" Then she finally noticed his bruises. "Oh, my God! What happened?"

"I bumped into someone's fist in an alley. Unfortunately, my face broke the fall," Jack answered as he finally moved back to the bed and sat on the edge of it.

Amanda crossed over to him, "You poor, poor baby ..." And then *boom*—she tripped on a chair and fell face first on the floor. Jack did everything he could to stifle his laughter. Funniest move ever. But he quickly got hold of himself and helped her up onto the bed.

He propped up her head on a pillow. "How much did you drink?"

"Enough to ask if I could use your sofa for the night," she said, looking up at him pitifully. "There're no vacancies left in Venice, Jack, and I can't bear another night in…"

"Look, it's the least I can do," Jack interrupted. "Besides, it's a big room, and I could use the company."

He wrapped some ice in a towel and put it on her forehead. She winced, still plastered but adorable. "I brought you a present," she said. "It's in the bag. Go ahead, open it."

Jack grabbed the shopping bag. He fished inside pulling out a *silver jewelry box with pearl inlays on the top and bottom*. Jack turned it from side to side to study it, eyeing it confused. He had no idea what to make of it. "It's, ah … it's very unique. What am I supposed to do with it?"

Amanda finally realized what he was holding.

"Not that," she said giggling. "The card at the bottom."

Jack rolled his eyes, retrieving a *business card* from the bottom of the bag.

"It's from the shop across from the place where I bought the jewelry box."

"So?"

"It's an *antique* jewelry shop," she clarified. "The night clerk thinks the owner sold your ring."

Jack grinned. A grin one would recognize had they known him for the fifteen years he'd been a cop in Boston. It was his *go-to* grin, the one he sported every time an investigation started breaking his way. Jack quickly checked his watch. Then he frowned.

"I know, sorry. The owner won't be in until nine tomorrow morning," she said, knowing he was itching to find where the lead might take him.

"Shit. That's twelve hours," Jack said disappointed.

She laid back, still woozy, staring up at him. "People can get crazy in Venice with that kinda time on their hands... How about you, Jack? Feel like getting a little crazy?"

Now here's the thing—Amanda had a body one might call fashionably *athletic.* Muscular in tone, tanned and well oiled. But it had a sensuality to it one would usually find only on thinner, more delicate women. Either way, Jack struggled with his passion. The insanity of having an overwhelming attraction to two different women in the *same* room within a few days' time was not lost on him. But his fantasy night with Claudia had gone unrequited and his life had been turned upside down. So he decided to go with this. Hell, after everything that had happened, he deserved it. He looked into her eyes, embracing the lottery he felt he might have just won. "Just what did you have in mind?" he asked.

She jumped up abruptly and gave her answer.

"Taking a walk," she announced.

"Huh?" Jack said incredulously.

Chapter X

In the distance, the lights of San Marco twinkled across the oily black lagoon. A gondola floated to a stop next to a landing beneath a seventeenth century brick wall. Amanda and Jack climbed out of the gondola as the gondolier steadied the vessel.

Jack eyed the fortress-like wall and their mysterious surroundings impatiently. "Mind telling me where we are?"

"The Villa Eden, the most enchanted garden in Venice. The Royals used to take their mistresses here." Amanda's lips formed a mischievous grin. "It's supposed to be haunted."

"How romantic," Jack replied disappointed. "A moonlight stroll with a bunch of dead adulterers."

Jack paid the gondolier and started to follow her up a staircase leading to a tall iron gate. Amanda turned when she heard him trudging up the chipped travertine stairs behind her.

"Wait!" she said childlike. "Count to twenty-first."

Jack shook his head. The Gondolier shrugged, murmuring, "Ahh, amore."

As he dug his oar into the water, Jack called out after him, "Pick us up in an hour?"

The gondolier watched Amanda moving up the steps. Without turning, she held up three fingers to the gondolier with one hand while the other started removing her jacket. The gondolier smiled. "Three hours," he said to Jack with a wink. "Life is short, signor. Why rush it?"

With that, the Gondolier pulled his oar through the water deftly pushing his left foot off the wall of the garden. In seconds, the gondola disappeared into the night.

When Jack turned back toward the stairs, Amanda was gone. But the gate was open now, and it beckoned.

AFTER A LONG and somewhat exhausting moonlit *treasure hunt* through the garden's misty topiary and statuary-filled maze, Jack stopped to catch his breath in the shadows. The leaves in the trees were softly rustling their siren-like song above him.

Jack scanned the garden for any sign of

Amanda. She had eluded him so far, which he assumed was her intention. The lower part of his body was still aroused by the chase, but the part of him that lived between his ears was getting impatient, perhaps even pissed. It was then he spotted her shirt draped over a statue of a lion about twenty meters away. He looked beyond it and caught a fleeting glimpse of Amanda standing beneath a colonnade. In an instant, she had vanished. But not before Jack realized she was naked. His body quickly reassembled its joint alliance and he resumed pursuit.

As Jack wound through more topiary, he found Amanda's pants on a statue of Bacchus with her lace panties wrapped around the god's face. He scanned the grounds and caught a glimpse of her naked body streaking backlit across an archway. It was cold, but Jack's temperature was rising.

He stalked her, weaving through an obstacle course of broken statues and gnarled trees. His feet splashed through a pond, slowing him down, allowing him to realize he'd lost her again. All of a sudden, he felt ridiculous. This was insane. He stopped dead in his tracks.

"I hate games, Amanda!" Jack yelled.

He looked for her in every direction. He heard a noise behind him. He rushed over to a

clearing. He spotted the back of a large fountain. Saw something move inside it.

Jack edged toward it cautiously. The moonlight cast an eerie blue shadow across the marble. The gentle wind was a haunting chorus to
the sound of the fountain's rushing water. Jack
finally reached the statue.

It towered above him. Jack immediately realized what it was—a three-hundred-year-old
reproduction of *Venus standing on the half
shell.* Water flowed from the top of the stone
goddess down onto a goddess who was even
more beautiful—*Amanda.*

The water cascaded off her hair, flowed
past the *black onyx cameo* on her neck, and
made its way down her breasts. It caressed every bump on her naked skin, a skin titillated and
erect from the chill of the midnight air.

Jack moved toward her hungrily. Lightning
had struck twice. And so far, he had survived
it.

Chapter XI

The phone rang indelicately. Its shrill alarm knifed through a dawn still held at bay by the thick velvet curtains protecting the darkness inside Room 502. The room's floor was cluttered with loose clothing, parted with in a hurry, leaving a trail wet with passion ending on top of the bed where Amanda still lay naked, entwined in silk sheets.

Relentless, the ringing continued. Amanda rubbed her palms over her face trying in vain to kill the hangover. She finally opened her eyes, searching for Jack. She smiled, finding a note from him on the pillow. Thinking it must be him on the phone, she finally answered. "Hi," she murmured sexily.

There was a long pause on the other end. Eventually, a woman's flustered voice responded. "I must have the wrong room … I was trying to reach Jack Sands."

"You have the right room," Amanda offered matter-of-factly. "He's gone out. Can I take a message?"

There was another long pause on the other end. Kate's voice finally resumed, clipped and irritated. "No. Just tell him his *wife* called."

Click. Kate hung up. Amanda winced, then put down the phone, and picked up Jack's note, reading it aloud.

Gone to the jewelry shop. Didn't want to wake you. Enjoyed the 'walk.' It's been awhile—Jack

Amanda folded the note and leaned back against the headboard to consider it. The words were sweet, but the bitterness in Kate's voice rendered them sour in effect.

Amanda finally forced herself out of bed. She grabbed her clothes off the floor on her way to the drapes. As she flung them open, the sun forced its way in, showering her nakedness with a warm, golden light. She turned for a look at herself in the etched, full-length mirror. Amanda liked what she saw.

IT WAS NEARLY NOON. Last night's carnival goers were just crawling out of their rooms and onto the campo where, a day earlier, Amanda found the shop whose clerk remembered selling the ring. Amanda was outside in front of it talking to its owner. He pointed her in the direction of a small trattoria on the campo.

Once there, Amanda's eyes scanned a maze of umbrellas covering tables in the trattoria on the Campo Santa Maria. She finally spotted Jack. He was on his cellphone, but he hung up as he saw her approaching his table. Amanda looked fresh and ravishing despite being ravished the night earlier. She was all smiles. "Miss me?" she said.

"Definitely," Jack said, still hungry for her.

"Good. Wanna tell me about the *wife*?" she demanded, her smile vanishing.

The question caught him off guard, but Jack quickly put it together. He answered crisply with eyes that, for the moment at least, seemed apologetic and genuine. "Separated. We're getting divorced."

Her smile returned. "OK, that works. Not a real resume builder, but I'll go with it. She called this morning."

"Was she upset?" he asked concerned.

"A bit. Were you straight with her?"

"Always. But we shared a lot together. Kate's a good person, and I would never want to hurt her."

Amanda studied Jack a beat. His answer surprised her, the almost naïve nobility of it. It was the kind of answer most men in her past might have given but never meant. But this man in front of her, somehow, she believed and admired him for it.

"If you were straight with her, she'll get over it," she assured, running her hand through his hair as she would a child. "It's the cheating women can't stand, Jack. It's murder on a relationship."

She seemed to say this from a pained knowingness, an apparent victim of wounds that cut deep. Not one to be burdened by oppressive memories, Amanda's mood quickly turned upbeat.

"What did you find out about the ring?" she asked as she eyed the jewelry shop across the square.

"You were right. The owner sold it three years ago."

Amanda sat down and nuzzled up to him. "What would you do without me?"

"Have a lot fewer orgasms in fountains."

"Fountains were just for openers, Jack," she answered sexily. "Who bought the ring?"

"Ready for this one?"

Amanda nodded.

"Vitale Donato. One of Bellini's partners."

"Jesus… You think he did it?"

"Maybe," Jack allowed. "Meanwhile, I need you to do a little research. Dig up what you can on Transitalia."

Amanda nodded, considering it. "Okay. But what's in it for me?"

He stared at her warmly, gently pulling the hair back off her face. "The *exclusive*. Remember?"

She smiled and kissed him softly on the cheek. Jack grinned almost boyishly. Whatever they had between them, he was getting lost in it. That, and the rush that came from knowing he was inching his way toward solving a murder.

Chapter XII

The Arsenale on the edge of Venice was massive and foreboding. It was still on its feet more than 700 years after its enormous brick bacinis housed the shipyards that helped the Venetians become the merchants who mastered the world. And perhaps, had it not been for the military prowess and audacity of Napoleon, Venice might have remained so. Instead, she and her Arsenale now catered to tourists and the odd yachtsman whose hull was in need of repair. Nonetheless, some diehard Venetians still kept their offices there. The Arsenale reminded them of Venice's powerful past, an iconic mojo from antiquity, a tonic for aging titans.

One such titan was the motivation for Jack's visit to the Arsenale that afternoon. Vitale Donato had his office there. Donato was the oldest partner in Transitalia, Claudia's husband's multi-billion dollar shipping company. But more importantly, Donato was the man who bought the Fortuny ring.

And now, Jack had found him. Jack was high above a tanker undergoing repairs in an Arsenale dry dock. Holding a pair of binoculars, Jack watched Donato as he was talking to someone familiar at the bottom of the shipyard—*Captain Lucca Giovanni*. Jack watched as Donato handed Lucca an *envelope*.

Collecting some payola, hey, Lucca? Spineless, corrupt, little bastard, Jack thought to himself.

Jack heard a noise behind him. He turned quickly finding the *large man* who had assaulted him the night earlier. This encounter promised to be a little different as the large man was pointing a gun at him.

"You have a short memory, Signor Sands," the large man grunted in broken English.

Jack started to walk over to him calmly, the binoculars dangling at his side.

"I got a long memory, pal. But I got a helluva short temper."

With that, Jack swung the binoculars like a mace onto the large man's hand. The gun flew to the ground. In an instant, Jack pounced on his assailant, hungry for revenge.

Jack opened with a hard knee to the large man's groin. Then a left shin into his back, followed by two lightning jabs into the large man's throat and face. The large man crumpled into a writhing ball on the ground.

Jack pulled a Transitalia identity badge from the large man's lapel and read his name out loud. "*Salvatore Pisani*. Well, nice to meet you, *Sal*," Jack said as the large man started to come to. Jack reached down forcefully and grabbed Sal by the lapels. "This is so you should know respect." Then Jack head-butted him hard.

The large man fell unconscious to the concrete.

Jack resumed watching Donato. Donato had just split off from Lucca and was heading toward the Transitalia offices on the western side of the Arsenale. Jack followed.

DONATO was the chief financial officer of Transitalia. In the early days, when the shipping company he started with Carlo Bellini was in its infancy, they only had one small tanker. It was Donato who found the money to expand. Carlo had family in Naples. They knew some *banking interests* there. In those days, that was the only euphemism used for the Camorra. Nowadays, Neapolitans call it what it is. Obfuscation aside, the Camorra happily bankrolled Transitalia's expansion. In turn, they received legitimacy and a healthy interest payment on their money. Those payments were always made on time, and the fact that all three partners were still breathing was a living testament to their punctuality.

Jack knew none of this as he brazenly walked through the front doors leading into Donato's suite of offices wearing Sal's badge on his lapel. He made his way toward Donato's inner office passing three desks and three secretaries, each eyeing him curiously. Then he passed the *small man*, the one who had worked him over in the alley previously.

The small man eyed Jack in alarm and jumped to his feet. Jack shoved the palm of his hand in the small man's face and pushed him back into the chair. Before the small man could recover, Jack pushed through Donato's inner office door.

Jack found Donato behind his desk in a meeting with two elderly women. Donato was stunned by the intrusion, and the women seemed appropriately offended.

"Morning, Signor Donato," Jack said brazenly. "I'm afraid I don't have an appointment."

The small man rushed into the office brandishing a handgun that was pointed in Jack's direction.

"You don't want to do that, tiny," Jack said calmly. "It's daylight and these little ladies here are witnesses."

Donato signaled the small man to put away his gun. Then he turned impatiently to Jack. "May I ask the purpose of your visit here, Mr. Sands?"

"Sure you can, Vitale. I just want a few words with you regarding Claudia Bellini," Jack said as he watched the small man reluctantly put away his weapon.

"Perhaps later," Donato answered dismissively. "As you can see, I'm a busy man."

"My questions pertain to a little item you were looking for at the scene of a murder," Jack explained. "A Fortuny ring?"

Donato squirmed. The women stared at him confused. Donato said something to them in Italian then he turned back to Jack. "We can talk outside," Donato said begrudgingly.

The small man escorted Jack into the corridor and started to frisk him. Jack allowed it.

JACK AND DONATO held their private conversation while walking through an abandoned ancient bacini at the edge of the Arsenale. By now, Sal had recovered and was standing alongside the small man in the distance watching Jack and their boss. Donato was typically Venetian, his hands saying more than his words. And as he discussed Claudia Bellini with Jack, his hands were working overtime.

"Of course, I hated her. She was easy to hate," Donato admitted impatiently. "But your allegations are preposterous. She was an irritation. No more, no less."

"But she was trying to force Carlo to sell, wasn't she?" Jack said, studying Donato's eyes. "Maybe it was more convenient to get her out of the way."

Donato stopped and shook his head annoyed.

"Look around you, Mr. Sands." Donato gestured at the massive brick walls surrounding them. "You're standing in the same bacini where, centuries ago, my forefathers built the ships that made the Venetians trade masters of the world. From this, we built Transitalia, the fifth largest shipping company on the planet. No man, no foreign corporation, and certainly no *woman* could ever threaten that."

"Unless your partners were to be persuaded otherwise."

"Our charter ensures that all partners must

agree before any of us can sell their shares," Donato said smugly. "So you see, Mr. Sands, even if Claudia persuaded Carlo to sell, he couldn't sell without my permission."

Jack was a fast read when it came to liars and Donato seemed sincere. Jack was buying into Donato's innocence. Still, he pressed.

"If you had nothing to do with this, why did you have your men work me over?" Jack said, indicating the large and small man in the distance.

"I didn't. They also work for my partners. Take it up with them. And as for your ring, I purchased it years ago. As a *gift*."

"That's a convenient alibi."

"It's the truth!" Donato said aggravated. "Look, Mr. Sands, I'm a reasonable man, but your allegations and threatening letters are becoming a nuisance."

"I never sent you any letters," said Jack thrown.

"I've no patience for liars, Mr. Sands! I received your letter this—"

Suddenly, *two gloved hands* grabbed Donato's head from behind a wall!

Like lightning, the shiny blade of a *knife* savagely sliced Donato's neck.

Donato screamed, choking on his own

blood as his assassin escaped into the shadows.

Jack was in shock. He raced toward Donato as a SHOT rang out. Jack dove to the ground. Sal and the small man were firing, running toward him, eyeing Donato lying lifeless in a pool of blood, and thinking Jack was the cause of it.

Jack jumped up as Sal's next shot pummeled the ground beneath him. Jack leapt to the safety of a wall and started to run. Sal and the small man gave chase.

The three men raced through the ruins. Sal barked into a walkie-talkie. Within seconds, Jack was encircled by Arsenale security.

A guard brandishing an Uzi screamed at Jack to stop. Surrounded, Jack finally stopped and dropped to his knees. He placed his hands behind his head as the guards descended upon him.

The small man lunged at him and began punching Jack in the face. The guards peeled the small man off him. The guards flex-cuffed Jack and dragged him away.

Chapter XIII

Carabinieri headquarters throbbed with activity that day. It wasn't often that its three-hundred-year-old walls held a murderer. Let alone, a murderer with an American passport.

Jack was seated at an interrogation table while Lucca paced above him puffing on a cigar. Jack batted away the smoke.

"I'm sorry. Does the smoke bother you?" Lucca said cynically.

"Immensely," Jack answered coughing.

"Well, that's the way I feel about murder," Lucca fired back.

"We've been over and over this, Lucca! I am not a total idiot. I wouldn't waltz in there and murder Donato in front of two of his men!"

"If you didn't kill him, then who did?"

"I told you! It happened in an instant. I didn't get a clear look at the guy! For all I know, it could have been you! You were there this morning… collecting your bribe!"

"What??" Lucca said offended.

"Oh, Jeezus, let's get real here, Lucca, don't try and play me. I saw Donato hand you an envelope on the dry dock."

Lucca glared at Jack a moment then took an envelope from his pocket. He pulled out the letter inside it and shoved it in front of Jack.

"Hardly a bribe, Mr. Sands," Lucca said firmly. "Donato was giving me the letter you threatened him with."

The letter was written in English. Jack read it out loud.

I know your secret. You'll die trying to keep it.

Jack threw down the letter frustrated and rolled his eyes at Lucca. "You seriously think I wrote this? Way too cheesy and ridiculously incriminating. I'm not a murderer, Lucca, but if I were, I wouldn't be such a goddamn amateur at it."

Lucca picked up the letter, eyeing Jack dismissively. "Tell that to the magistrate. You'll have sufficient time to think of an alibi in your cell."

"*Cell?* You can't be serious about charging me with this!"

Lucca leaned down and got right in Jack's

face. "Look into these eyes, Mr. Sands. Don't they look like the eyes of a serious man?"

Jack slumped in his chair as Rizzo, Lucca's weasel-faced subordinate, answered a knock on the office door.

Lucca turned to find a distinguished, elderly Venetian in a charcoal gray suit clutching a leather briefcase. The man had a whispered conversation with Lucca and Rizzo in Italian.

The discussion escalated. Lucca's temper flared. Lucca slammed his hand angrily against the wall then he turned back to Jack. "Get out," Lucca said sharply.

"What??" Jack asked in shock.

"*Get out!*" Lucca repeated angrily. "You're free to go."

Jack jumped on it. He almost flew out the door. Lucca blocked him with a firm arm against Jack's chest. "Stay close to your hotel, Mr. Sands. I wouldn't want anything to *happen* to you."

Lucca lowered his arm bitterly. He and Rizzo glared at Jack as they watched him disappear out the door.

Outside in the corridor, Jack walked confused alongside the man in the gray suit. The man's name was Paolo Ziani, and he was one of the finest, most expensive criminal attorneys in the Veneto.

"Nobody actually saw you do it. No weapon was found at the scene and the letter was typed and unsigned," Ziani explained. "A man like Donato had many enemies. The Magistrate conceded the carabinieri had no authority to hold you."

"You're an excellent attorney, Mr. Ziani," Jack said gratefully. "How much do I owe Giorgio for retaining you?"

"*Giorgio*? I don't understand."

"Giorgio Sanudo, the curator of the Accademia. Didn't he—"

"I was hired by Signora Parks," Ziani interrupted. "She was quite devastated by your arrest."

Ziani looked toward the lobby below them and indicated Amanda pacing nervously near the main entrance.

Amanda beamed relieved catching sight of Jack. Jack took Ziani's business card and thanked him profusely for his services. He headed toward Amanda in the lobby.

ON THE FONDAMENTA outside carabinieri headquarters, Jack hugged Amanda warmly. He finally pulled back and eyed her gratefully.

"I owe you for this. Thank you."

Amanda seemed a little shaken. "When I didn't hear from you, I looked for you at the hotel. When Rossini told me you were arrested, I was so worried. Scared shitless for you, actually. You sure you're all right?"

"I'm doing a helluva lot better than Donato."

"Maybe it's time to get out of Venice, Jack? Claudia's gone. There's nothing you can do about it. It's not worth risking—"

"*No.*" Jack shook his head undeterred. "They're playing me, Amanda. Trying to stop me from finding her killer. It's no fun unless I get to play back."

He put his arm around her, and they headed down the Fondamenta toward the Palazzo Giovanni. Jack stopped short seeing Sal, the large man, watching them from a motoscafo cruising by at the edge of the canal. Jack grabbed Amanda, and they slipped down a narrow calle anxious to escape the large man's gaze.

Chapter XIV

Jack was inside the bathroom of Room 502 washing off his face. He was naked, except for a towel wrapped around his waist, talking to Amanda through the closed bathroom door.

"Donato said he bought the ring as a gift.

"A gift for who?" Amanda asked from inside the room.

"I don't know. Some guy severed his arteries before I could ask him." Jack dried his face and walked back into the room. He stopped startled, seeing someone half-naked in a *gold cape* and a *carnival mask with three faces*.

The costumed interloper turned out to be Amanda. She was trying on the outfit, staring at its impact in the mirror.

"What do you think?" she asked, her voice hollow, distorted by the mask. "I bought it on the Rialto."

Amanda took off the mask and smiled. Then she took off the cape. She was naked, except for a thin lace top.

Obviously, Jack had seen her body before, but the vision of it hadn't lost its potency. Jack just stood there at a loss for words. Amanda smiled mischievously.

"C'mon, you're all worked up. I've got something to relax you."

Jack knew where this was going, and as much as he wanted to go there, the day's activities had taken their toll on him.

"I don't know if now's the time, Amanda."

"Now's all there is, Jack," She moved over to him and gently grabbed his arm. "I promise it'll help you think better."

OUTSIDE ON THE TERRACE, the sun had almost set and the tall topiary blocked any of its remaining rays from reaching the shallow marble pond in the center of the terrace garden.

Weaving through the maze of topiary, Amanda led Jack to the pond. She had thrown on a robe but hadn't bothered to close it. Had any guests in Room 504 been able to see them, Amanda wouldn't have cared. Luckily for Jack, and what was left of his modesty, Room 504 was empty that night, so what was about to happen would go unseen by any of the other hotel guests. Only the pigeons were in attendance, and they watched as Amanda and Jack finally reached the edge of the pond.

Jack eyed the pond curiously though he'd seen it many times in the past. It was square and about a foot deep. At its head was a small, angled urn, which normally acted as a fountain to recirculate the water in the pond. Only tonight, the pond's water seemed *oily*. It glistened in the moonlight as Jack dipped his hand into the viscous fluid and pressed down on the white cotton lounge cushion submerged beneath it.

"You've got to be kidding?" he said, guessing what she was up to.

"Lay down on top of the cushion. I'm gonna work the tension out of your muscles." Amanda motioned Jack into the pond.

Jack smelled the fluid from the pond dripping down his fingers. "What is this stuff?"

"Secret Venetian massage technique. Glycerin and lilac oil. I had the maid smuggle it in." Amanda said, dropping her robe. "C'mon. Get in."

Jack dropped his towel apprehensively and slipped into the oil. He immersed half his body in it, lying on top of the submerged cushion. Amanda climbed on top of him and straddled his hips. She ran her hands sensually up and down his sides.

"Like it?" she asked smiling.

Jack just sighed with pleasure. Every part of him was aroused by the unapologetic eroticism of Amanda's technique. The glycerin and lilac oil were working their magic. Jack never felt better.

Amanda started massaging his legs. The oil glistened on his skin as her hand crept up his thigh. Her hand stopped where a woman's hand would normally stop in that situation and began massaging what a hand would normally find there. Jack's brief serenity evaporated giving way to full-blown passion. He tugged on the only thing she was wearing, her lace top, and as it fell away, he pulled her down on top of him.

The pigeons and the statues on the terrace looked on as they began to make love. The pond seemed like such a natural setting for a sexual fantasy such as this that one had to wonder if it weren't the architect's original intention. Jack and Amanda were lost in each other. He barely opened his eyes. And when he did, he stopped abruptly, catching sight of—

The *chambermaid* standing inside the room watching them. She had a bundle of magazines and documents in her arms. Her fascination with the copulating couple gave way to embarrassment. She put the documents on a table and ran out of the room.

Jack shook his head, smiling

"Why'd you stop? I was *so* close…" Amanda demanded, staring down at him frustrated and out of breath.

"It was the maid," Jack answered, nodding to the window. "She brought magazines."

"Oh, God. I forgot to lock the door," she said, still out of breath. "It's the Transitalia material you wanted. A research assistant at St. Mark's library promised he'd send it over. I feel horrible."

"Don't feel bad," Jack said, grabbing his towel and climbing out of the pond. "She looked like she enjoyed it,"

"I'll bet," Amanda responded, climbing out herself. "She's always watching you, Jack. I think she has a bit of a crush on you. Maybe the next time we should ask her to join us?"

Jack just stared at her as she put on her robe and walked inside. *Was she serious or just a little jealous?* Jack wondered. He couldn't read her and that was half his fascination with her. He started to walk in after her when he caught sight of a *man* standing in the square across from the Palazzo. The man was watching them from the shadows. Jack eyed him apprehensively then went back inside the room.

AN HOUR LATER, Jack was peeking through the curtains of Room 502 watching the same man lurking in the same square below. It looked as if it could be Rizzo. But Jack wasn't sure.

"He still out there?" Amanda asked from inside.

"Hasn't moved," Jack said nodding. "Pretty soon the pigeons will be nesting on him."

Jack moved from the window back to the bed where Amanda was leafing through printouts of the Transitalia research from St. Mark's library. Jack was holding one of the printouts in his hand. His eyes returned to what he had been reading.

"It says here the takeover offer for Transitalia is still on the table. The bidder is Bremencorp, heavy hitters in global transport."

"Maybe they're killing off the partners to get the company," Amanda replied, combing through the other research.

"No. Too obvious. But you're on the right track. I think it's definitely somebody on the inside, someone who wants to force a sale."

"But you said Claudia *wanted* to sell. Who would have a reason to kill her?"

"Carlo, for one. He hated her," Jack said. "Carlo had his new girlfriend, Franchesca. Maybe he wanted to get back his shares from Claudia."

"Why? So he could give them to Franchesca?"

"Maybe. Either way, he worked his whole life to build that company. She was gonna leave him and take half his share of it. If that's not motive, I don't know what is."

Amanda picked up a newspaper clipping and eyed a photo of the three Transitalia partners taken in the 90s. She studied it a while before she shook her head unconvinced.

"I don't know about this insider theory of yours, Jack," she said, showing him the photo. "None of these guys look like assassins."

"I worked homicide ten years in Boston before I quit the force. First thing you learn is that most murderers look like the guy next door."

"You were a cop?" she asked surprised.

Jack nodded. He seemed anxious to drop the subject. She sensed this and pressed on.

"*So*? Why'd you quit?"

Jack didn't answer. She kept pressing.

"C'mon, Jack. *Why'd you quit*?"

Jack finally relented.

"...I had the goods on a local mob lieutenant running guns out of the harbor," he recounted. "I was about to turn the evidence over to the D.A. when the mob boss found out about it. Obviously, it was in his best interest that it didn't happen. So he made some moves… asked me to bend over."

"And?"

"So I did ... I quit."

"Weird. I wouldn't expect that from you, Jack. You don't seem like the bend-over type."

"Yeah?" Jack answered, with a hint of aggravation in his voice. "Well, he already shot up my partner, and he informed me my wife was next on the list. So at the time, it seemed like a good idea."

"Okay. So what about now?"

Jack glared at her. "Does it look like I'm bending over for this one, Amanda?"

Amanda backed off. Jack finally looked at the photo she was holding in her hand.

Something snapped. Jack grabbed it for a closer look. His eyes widened.

"Jesus ..." he gasped, and then he quickly started dressing like a man on a mission.

"Jack? What is it?" she asked confused.

Jack slipped on his shoes and headed out the door without turning. "I'll be right back."

With that, he was out the door. On his way,

he brushed past a waiter wheeling in a cart laden with the appetizers and champagne that Amanda had ordered previously.

The waiter left, and Amanda found herself alone. She stared at the newspaper photo wondering what revelation Jack had found in it.

The photo seemed harmless enough. It was a jovial black and white picture of Torelli, Donato, and Bellini with their arms around each other taken in the lobby of the Hotel Giovanni.

Now Amanda's eyes widened when she finally figured out what triggered Jack's haste—

It was the familiar piece of jewelry one of them was wearing on his finger. Only it wasn't Donato. It was Torelli. Torelli was wearing the *Fortuny ring.*

Chapter XV

The top floor of the Giovanni was private. There were only a couple of rooms. One was rarely booked, routinely reserved for foreign dignitaries and heads of state. The other was reserved for the manager's residence and Rossini was grateful to have it.

Rossini had spent thirty years as an employee of the hotel in various capacities but had never managed to save enough for his own apartment. And even if he had, it would have been difficult to part with the view from the upper floor of the Giovanni. It was one of the only places in Venice where you could get a peek of the Rialto and St. Marks from the same vantage point. And it was high enough up where you could do so in quiet as the noise off the Grand Canal did not disturb you there. But tonight, the incessant knocking on the front door did.

Rossini opened the door that Jack's knuckles had been rapping against. He was surprised and a little annoyed by the late night visit. Nonetheless, he politely invited Jack inside.

"The night manager said you'd be in. Sorry for the intrusion," Jack said, walking inside. "But we have to talk."

Rossini responded with his usual diplomacy. "It's no intrusion at all. I was just taking in the view."

Rossini offered Jack a cognac while gazing out the window. He eyed the dramatic *winged lion* on top of the column of Saint Mark towering above the Piazza San Marco.

"Magnificent, isn't it?" said Rossini. "Venice is the only city in the world where the lions fly and the pigeons walk."

"Well, actually, tonight I'm only interested in things that walk," Jack said, taking a sip of cognac. "Specifically, Antonio Torelli. Does he stay at your hotel?"

"Always," Rossini answered.

"Recently?"

"Of course. Signor Torelli has quite an appetite for female companionship. But he insists on discretion," Rossini explained with an insider's grin. "Especially in light of his past."

"Really?" Jack replied, his interest spiking. "What past is that?"

Rossini seemed reluctant to answer, at least

absent motivation. Jack caught on quickly. He pulled a hundred euro bill from his pocket and placed it inside an open silver box that was resting next to the bottle of cognac. Rossini closed the box delicately as Jack repeated, "What past is that?"

Rossini sat down and, with the wave of a hand, invited Jack to do the same. Then he proceeded to earn his gratuity.

"Regrettably, a past filled with accusations of murder," Rossini revealed.

Well worth the price of admission, Jack thought as he leaned closer to Rossini.

"Please continue."

"Continuing might lead to indiscretion," replied Rossini sheepishly."

"In my case, indiscretion will motivate generosity. So please go on," Jack prodded.

Rossini smiled, the light from his desk lamp seeming to twinkle off his signature toothy grin.

"Well, if you insist... Signor Torelli was having an affair with the wife of a former partner. Not a partner in Transitalia, mind you—at least not on this particular occasion," Rossini explained with a wink. "The two of them were caught in the act by the woman's husband. A fight ensued. The husband died by suffocation.

A plastic bag, if I'm not mistaken. The Magistrate ruled it an accident." Rossini paused briefly, filling his glass with more cognac. "Signor Torelli has had rather unfortunate luck with his partners' lovers—especially *Signora Bellini.*"

Rossini knew the effect this last little tidbit would have on Jack, and his decision to delay its reveal would probably earn him another hundred euros.

"You're telling me Torelli had an affair with Claudia?" Jack replied in shock, remembering Torelli's face and thinking the first time he saw it, how much it reminded him of a Pit Bull. A hopelessly ugly Pit Bull at that.

"Signor Torelli *tried,*" Rossini clarified. "In fact his attempt took place here at the hotel. But Signora Bellini rebuffed him. It caused quite a scandal."

"Was he in the hotel the day of the suicide?" Jack fired back quickly.

Rossini thought for a moment and then answered. "He wasn't registered. But it doesn't mean he wasn't here."

"What's that supposed to mean?"

"As I informed you, Signor Torelli desires his privacy. To ensure it, sometimes he'll enter the hotel by way of the passage.

"Passage? What passage?" Jack asked confused.

"The passage in the calle behind the palazzo. It bypasses the lobby. Many of the guests use it as a convenience. As often as you've stayed here, I'm surprised you don't know of it."

"Show me," Jack demanded as he pulled another hundred euro note from his wallet and placed it in Rossini's box He closed the lid to save Rossini the trouble.

"It would be my pleasure, Mr. Sands," Rossini replied, his grin in full bloom as the two of them stood and headed out the door.

THE PALAZZO GIOVANNI began its life five centuries earlier as the private residence of a middle-aged doge who was sick and dying years before other men similar in age and stature would normally die in the Veneto. The malady was cancer of the brain, brought about by syphilis, contracted early in life, and left untreated to the great delight of his heirs. The doge was determined to live life *fully* as he had always lived it, which necessitated a steady parade of young women, paid by the night for their services and, more importantly, their discretion. Discretion required them to enter the Giovanni unseen by others, especially the doge's family, namely his wife, so for this reason, and this reason alone, a secret passage was built at the base of the palazzo.

The passage's entrance was marked by a short iron gate in the middle of a narrow calle underneath the Giovanni's western wall. Rossini was standing in front of it with Jack who waited impatiently for Rossini to unlock the gate. The mechanism was rusty, but it finally clicked open. The thick iron gate creaked and groaned as Rossini swung it open while explaining the Cliff's Notes version of its origin to Jack.

"This was a private entrance from the piazza built by Doge Grimani in 1598. As I said earlier, most of our guests know of it. I apologize you haven't been told. All of our room keys work the lock."

Jack fished the key to Room 502 out of his pocket. He tried it in the lock. It worked. He poked his head inside the dimly lit, limestone passage asking, "Where's it lead?"

"To the second-floor portego," Rossini answered. "Directly across from your room."

Jack's mind raced. He quickly moved into the passage and disappeared from Rossini's sight.

The passage's musty corridor was dimly lit

by low wattage bulbs. Half of them needed re-placing. Jack was surprised at how filthy it was, not up to normal Giovanni standards for sure. But then again, its primary utility was on-ly of value to adulterers. And the odd murderer.

Jack finally emerged from the passageway through a thick wooden door on the second floor of the hotel. The floor was empty except for the *chambermaid* who Jack saw earlier. She smiled sexily as Jack walked toward Room 502. He found this odd at the time, especially in light of her embarrassment earlier, but he had things that were more pressing on his mind. He counted his steps across the portego. Fifteen in all, from the passage's exit to the door of Room 502. *A killer could cover that ground in ten seconds or less*, Jack thought as he swung open the door to Room 502.

Once back inside the room, Jack was exu-berant about his discovery.

"Torelli's our man," Jack declared. "Christ, it's brilliant! There's a special passage to this floor from the alley. He must've sneaked in unseen—murdered Claudia, then ..."

He finally took in the room. It was lit ro-mantically by candles that had almost melted away. The champagne bottle was nearly empty. Amanda was half-naked in the bed. He crossed over to her apologetically.

"Jesus, I'm sorry ... I didn't think it would take so long. I'll make it up to you."

Amanda curled away from him.

"Right … You just solved a murder case and now you can get romantic," she pouted.

"Just stay there, and I'll prove it to you. We'll pick up where we left off." Jack smiled and headed toward the bathroom.

Amanda perked and started straightening the bed.

Inside the bathroom, Jack undressed quickly. He wrapped himself in a towel, brushed his teeth, and splashed on some cologne. He took a moment to study his face. It was presentable. No. Better than presentable. He looked damned good that night. Confident, sexy and ready to celebrate. After all, he was sure he had just solved a murder. It was a simple matter now. Fill in a couple more blanks and present the evidence on a silver platter to Lucca.

Jack exited the bathroom and headed toward the bed. The candles had almost burnt out, but the light was still bright enough to reveal Amanda underneath the sheets. She was wearing the *triple-faced mask* and gold cape she had tried on earlier. Jack closed in on her hungrily

"Carnival time, eh, Amanda?" he said with a smile.

He reached the bed. She didn't move. He dropped his towel and climbed underneath the sheets from the bottom of the bed.

Jack snaked his way up her body. She groaned with pleasure, the outline of his body revealing exactly where he lingered.

The sheets rustled as he climbed further toward her chest. They both groaned as he finally pushed himself deep inside her and they resumed the rhythmic grind that was preempted in the fountain earlier.

"My, God, how do you stay so tight?" he moaned as the grind quickened, and with it, more erotic groaning. Jack allowed himself to get lost in it. All of his senses focused on his ecstasy and her body and not on the wall behind him, or he would have clearly seen—the *shadow of a knife.*

A shadowy figure was holding it, moving toward them on the bed.

Jack pumped harder and harder as the shadow of the knife got closer and closer. It finally raised, ready to strike as—

Click. Jack spun around hearing the flick of a cigarette lighter. A flame suddenly burned bright. The shadowy figure wasn't holding a knife, just a candle. A candle that was now lit, revealing the shadowy figure holding it— *Amanda*.

"Just thought you might want to see what you're doing," Amanda said calmly, standing behind him wearing a thin red lace robe.

Jack freaked. He turned back incredulous to the female body below him.

He ripped off the *triple-faced mask* for a look at who he had been having sex with.

It was the *chambermaid*!

"Are you crazy!! What the fuck!!" Jack yelled at Amanda as he recoiled from the bed.

Amanda stayed calm. She inched toward the bed and the naked chambermaid now lying awkwardly beneath her.

"Watch your language, Jack. You'll embarrass her."

Jack was speechless as Amanda let her thin lace robe slip off her shoulders revealing her naked body. The oil from the fountain was still glistening on her breasts.

Amanda locked eyes with Jack whose own eyes were frozen for the moment in confusion. Without looking at her, Amanda slid down next to the chambermaid who trembled with expectation.

Jack watched the chambermaid's hand as it

moved up Amanda's thigh. Amanda watched Jack as he vacillated between trepidation and arousal. Amanda shivered as the maid's hand finally reached its destination. Amanda reached out to Jack

"Come on, Jack," Amanda purred, rubbing her hand on his thigh. "I really don't mind," she said as she pulled him toward her. "Please stop pretending that you do."

Jack hesitated at first, but the temptation was overwhelming. He finally gave in.

Amanda wrapped her sensuous lips around his mouth as the chambermaid wrapped her serpentine legs around his back.

The three of them disappeared beneath the sheets and the subjects of the paintings lining the walls of Room 502 were treated to an erotic frenzy.

Chapter XVI

At dawn, the rising sun bathed the canopy above the Florentine bed in Room 502 with a soft winter light. The chambermaid was gone. Jack was awake staring at the ceiling as Amanda stirred in the bed beside him. She slid over and kissed him hungrily on the cheek. He didn't respond.

'Oh, come on, Jack" she said annoyed. "Let's not spoil this with false pretense. It's what you wanted, wasn't it? It's what *all* men want."

"Is it what *you* want?" Jack responded, finally turning to her.

She stared at him a moment, then rolled over on her side.

"I want the knight in the armor on the white horse who'll go easy on my heart and stay loyal to my bed," she answered, standing and putting on her robe. "But I went shopping for that model, and they just don't make them anymore. So I settle for a little variety."

"Maybe you shouldn't have settled," Jack said cynically. "Maybe you should've just kept shopping."

Amanda turned to him and smiled. It was almost a sad smile. "Why? Know where I can find a guy like that?"

Jack answered her with eyes so genuine it made her even sadder. "I got everything but the horse," he said.

Amanda just stared at him. His hair was tousled, his face sincere. He was anxious to atone for a night he now regretted. She found something in his face she had never known, perhaps something she'd been searching for her whole life—a confused nobility, a yearning to be loved. She wondered if the scarred past imprisoning her own heart would ever let her embrace a man such as this. She wrestled with it, her face starting to soften. But the moment was broken by a *knock* on the door.

She walked over to answer it.

"If it's the maid, tell her to try the guy in 504," Jack called out sarcastically as she finally reached the door.

Amanda peeked out the peephole then cracked open the door. A porter was outside with an envelope, which he promptly handed to her. She thanked the porter, shut the door and walked back to Jack, eyeing the envelope quiz-zically.

"What is it?" Jack asked

"Don't know. It's for you," she answered, handing it to him.

Jack opened the envelope. He pulled out the handwritten note inside it and read it. He looked up alarmed.

"Well? What is it?" Amanda asked.

Jack read the note aloud.

We'll settle this at the Palazzo Ducale.
Come at seven. Come alone.

Jack looked up unsettled. "It's signed *Antonio Torelli*." Jack handed her the note. He thought a moment then he quickly moved over to his suitcase.

"What do you think he wants?" Amanda asked rattled.

"Look, Torelli's the killer, and obviously, he must know I'm onto him," Jack said, start-ing to get dressed.

"It's a setup. You know that, right?" Amanda declared nervously. "You can't possi-bly be thinking about going to meet him."

"I'm done thinking about it." And with that, Jack headed to the door.

MOMENTS LATER, in the narrow calle beneath the western wall of the Giovanni, the iron gate to the secret passage creaked open and Jack emerged from the passage into the calle. Amanda followed him nervously.

"This is insane, Jack!"

"Look, Torelli will never tip his hand unless I show up alone. He'll spook if I play this any other way." Jack checked his watch. "Just give me thirty minutes before you call Lucca and tell him where I'm at."

"I got a real bad feeling about this, Jack," she said, moving close to him. "I don't want to lose you."

Jack cupped her face gently in his hands and stared softly into her eyes.

"And I don't want to be lost," he said, his words meant to reassure himself even more than they were supposed to reassure her.

Jack gave Amanda a passionate kiss good-bye and moved quickly down the alley calling out over his shoulder, "Make sure the tail thinks I'm still in the room."

Amanda nodded as Jack's voice echoed down the calle, and he disappeared from sight.

AT THE EDGE OF THE SMALL SQUARE

across the tiny canal beneath the window of Room 502, Rizzo, Lucca's subordinate, and the man Jack was watching earlier, was still on surveillance duty. He lit another cigarette standing above the twenty or so butts he had thrown to the cobblestones beneath him. He sipped on a cup of coffee between puffs, pacing agitated in the cold.

Rizzo looked like he'd been up all night. But then again, he had that kind of face. If one had lived with him, and no one ever had, they might have seen that same face when Rizzo woke up *refreshed*. It was a hard face to look at, but Rizzo wore it proudly.

Rizzo finally stopped pacing when he caught sight of someone standing in front of the east-facing window inside Room 502. It was Amanda. She was standing in front of the window half-naked wearing only her shirt, which was open, her breasts dangling in the dawn. Rizzo's cigarette dropped from his mouth as he *surveilled* her.

Amanda turned her back to him and dropped her shirt to the floor. Her naked ass pressed against the window as a pair of hands wrapped around her naked back and she began to kiss someone passionately.

Rizzo's eyes were glued to the show. So

much so, he didn't realize his coffee cup was tilting until its contents scalded his leg. He winced in pain, stifling a tiny, Rizzo-like scream, which the rats in the sewer nearby might have mistaken as a distress call from one of their own.

High up inside Room 502, Amanda was still *necking*, but it was definitely a solo procedure. She had her arms through the sleeves of one of Jack's shirts, and those arms were convincingly caressing her own back.

She was doing as Jack had asked, but the technique was providing some unexpected and welcome benefits. Amanda was taking great pleasure in getting Rizzo off, and she continued to do so much longer than the job required.

Chapter XVII

Half way across Venice, Jack slipped through the shadows until he reached the gated entrance at the bottom of the imposing *Palazzo Ducale*.

It was 6:30 in the morning. Most, if not all, carnival goers had just gone to bed and no respectable tourist would be up that early. Even the die-hard Croatians, who descended daily upon Piazza San Marco by the busloads, were absent.

Jack was alone when he slipped into the courtyard that morning, but he jumped back quickly seeing his old nemesis, Sal, the large man, keeping watch at the base of a steep marble staircase.

Jack eyed Sal unseen from behind a column. He spotted Sal nodding to someone higher up in the palazzo. Following Sal's gaze, he finally saw Torelli.

Torelli waited alone on the upper landing. He was pacing, as was his custom. Torelli was wired tight. The murder of his partner weighed heavily on him. Donato was the brains of Transitalia, Carlo Bellini the handsome face of it, but Torelli was its muscle. In the early days, when Transitalia was strapped for cash and they borrowed from the Camorra, Torelli was the one who managed the debt. Not the payment of it, but rather its consequences.

When the Camorra loaned money in those days, the Camorra's intention was not just to get back the principle, it was to become a *partner* in your business. And they wanted Transitalia bad. All of it. It was Torelli who changed their mind. To do that, he had to leverage his various political and Sicilian connections, and he had to make sure some intractable Camorrans died. So it was understandable that Donato's murder rattled him. Torelli ran security for the trio and Torelli's security had failed.

Jack was at the base of a narrow stairway in the rear of the Ducale now, picking the lock of a gate with a pen. The locked clicked and Jack inched the gate open enough so he could slip through. He moved stealthily up the stairs toward Torelli's position.

On the upper landing, Torelli waited impatiently, the lagoon's dramatic dawn coalescing behind him. Torelli kept Sal in sight. Sal was still standing watch below.

Halfway down the outer corridor of the landing, Jack crept toward Torelli from behind.

The approach was working perfectly until the edge of his foot creased the crumpled side of an aluminum can lying on the marble. The noise wasn't even loud enough to disturb a pigeon, they still slept soundly in their nests, but it was loud enough to alert Torelli. Torelli spun around. Not quickly enough to catch Jack ducking out of sight behind a column.

Out of Torelli's view, Jack eased his way down the outside passage on the upper landing. Jack caught a glimpse of Sal below. Sal was still waiting in the courtyard.

Jack inched forward. He was just a meter from the spot where he saw Torelli standing. He edged around a column to get a closer look at Torelli. Jack jumped back panicked when he realized Torelli had vanished.

Jack's breathing quickened as he turned frantically looking for Torelli. It was then that the butt of Torelli's gun smashed into the side of Jack's neck. It sent Jack crashing backward into the column.

Torelli seemed to come out of nowhere. But here he was and the barrel of his .45 was pressed forcefully against Jack's cheek.

"Come to kill me too, Mr. Sands?" Torelli said angrily, frisking Jack while he kept the gun on him.

"Look, I came here unarmed like you wanted. I have nothing to hide," Jack answered, still dazed from the initial blow.

Torelli confirmed Jack wasn't carrying. He backed away a step glaring at Jack while still keeping the gun on him. "For your sake, I would stay very still, Mr. Sands, like the granite relics around you, or you just might become one."

Jack nodded and Torelli whistled to Sal below. Sal looked up alarmed and started racing toward them up the winding marble staircase.

Torelli moved back to Jack. "How did you know I'd be here?" Torelli asked confused.

Jack eyed Torelli cynically. "Laying it on a little thick, aren't you, Torelli? You know why I'm here. You had this delivered to the hotel."

Torelli's aim firmed as Jack slowly reached into his jacket pocket and pulled out the note. "It's even written on your stationary," Jack said, handing the note to Torelli.

Torelli grabbed it and read it. Then he threw it to the ground aggravated. "This is nonsense. I never sent it. What possible reason would I have?"

Jack was thrown by how Torelli was playing this, but he decided to play along. "The *ring*. The Fortuny ring Donato gave you. You were looking for it under the bed in Room 502 the night after Claudia was murdered. You figured out that I found it a day later when I stayed in the room."

Torelli's face went pale. "That little tramp," he murmured.

"What?" Jack said confused.

"*Franchesca*," Torelli barked back. "I gave her the ring more than a year ago. She wore it on a chain around her neck."

"Jesus," said Jack, eyeing him incredulous. "You're a helluva cocksman, Torelli. You were also having an affair with Carlo's mistress?"

Torelli's mind was racing, trying to put it together. "Franchesca and I were involved long before she and Carlo ever met. Franchesca called my secretary last night. She told me to meet her here. She said it was urgent."

Before Jack even had time to process this, Torelli spun around suddenly, hearing footsteps down the corridor.

They didn't belong to Sal. They belonged to someone wearing a *black cape* and the familiar *assassin's carnival mask*. And that someone was holding a 9mm automatic aimed at Torelli.

Torelli lunged at Jack grabbing him by his throat "You son of a bitch! You set me up!!" he screamed.

Torelli spun Jack around using him as a shield between himself and the Assassin. Torelli shoved his gun angrily against Jack's temple. The Assassin kept moving toward them forcefully, the 9mm still raised.

"Move any closer, and I'll kill him!" Torelli yelled.

The Assassin didn't care. The Assassin raised the gun and aimed. Jack struggled frantically to escape Torelli's grip.

Crack. A *shot whizzed* by Jack's head and pierced Torelli's shoulder.

Sal finally reached the top of the stairs and raced toward them from the opposite corridor. His view of the melee was blocked by the long row of thick marble columns.

A hundred yards away, Torelli stumbled wounded to the ground. He fired two wild shots at Jack as he went down. Jack jumped on him. He tried to get the gun away from Torelli to protect himself as the Assassin was still coming.

The Assassin resumed fire relentlessly.

Three more shots pummeled Torelli's body. The Assassin took aim at Jack but ducked quickly into the shadows as Sal finally arrived at the scene waving his gun, crazed and out of breath.

Sal started firing at Jack. Jack leapt behind a column for safety. "I didn't shoot him," Jack yelled. "Goddammit, I didn't shoot him!!"

Sal finally reached Torelli. Torelli was dead. Sal spun around. The Assassin had long since vanished, an assassin Sal had never even seen. In Sal's mind, the killer was Jack, which, in retrospect, Jack would realize was the Assassin's intention. Sal spotted part of Jack's leg poking out from behind a column. Sal raised his gun angrily and fired. He tore after Jack like a maniac, grunting and yelling like a crazed grizzly.

Jack ran for his life, weaving in and out of the columns.

At the top of the staircase, Jack tore down the stairs, bounding down them, three by three, toward the gate below.

Sal was only a few yards behind him. Jack fumbled with the penknife to pick the lock. Sal fired a round that ricocheted off the wall just inches above him.

Jack finally swung open the gate. He

slipped outside and broke off the penknife in the lock. He slammed the gate shut and raced off.

Sal reached the gate. He couldn't get it open. He started to climb over the iron fencing.

A hundred yards away, Jack rounded a corner into a small campi that was beginning to fill with tourists.

Jack burst through the crowd. He stopped, seeing two carabinieri who were obviously responding to the shots that were fired at the Palazzo Ducale.

Jack started moving toward them. Then he hesitated, realizing the carabinieri would pin the shooting on him.

Jack bolted away seeing Sal catching sight of him in the distance.

Safely out of sight of the carabinieri, Jack sprinted toward the Piazza San Marco.

Chasing after Jack, Sal pushed through a group of tourists, knocking down an old woman in the process. The woman's young son kicked Sal as he passed, causing Sal to stumble. This slowed Sal down enough that he didn't spot Jack as he slipped away into the crowded piazza.

Safely hidden in the swelling throng that was now filling the Piazza San Marco, Jack finally caught his breath. He spotted three more carabinieri approaching from the eastern side of the piazza. Jack spun around nervously and spotted Sal approaching from the west.

Jack pushed through the crowd and slipped down a narrow calle at the edge of the piazza. The carabinieri didn't see him. But Sal did. Sal barreled toward Jack.

Jack's legs suddenly slammed to a stop. He stared back at Sal frantically. Jack had taken a wrong turn. He was boxed in. The calle was a dead-end, and Jack would soon suffer the same fate. Jack searched for a way out. He spotted an open door ten feet in front of him. He slipped inside it.

Bad move. Jack stumbled into a narrow staircase so steep that you needed to be a goat to climb it. Jack was out of options. So he took the only one he had. He bounded up the marble stairs.

Seconds later, he heard Sal burst through the door below. Jack quickened his pace as Sal struggled up the stairs beneath him. Sal fired a round an inch away from Jack's head as Jack neared the top.

Jack finally reached the door at the top of the staircase and swung it open. He raced outside, stopping abruptly, seeing he was trapped.

Jack finally realized where he was.

He was standing on top of the famous *bell tower* high above the Piazza San Marco. It was about sixty feet square, dominated by a huge bronze bell with two bronze statues of knights with bronze hammers that struck the bell on the hour. The bell tower was the one Venetian icon that every tourist was familiar with, especially Jack, for he'd been to the top of it just four years earlier. An exclusive guided tour reserved only for Venice's elite. The steep staircase leading to the bell was legendary, at minimum unforgettable, but today, Jack's haste had clouded his memory. And until just now, he had forgotten where he was. And hearing Sal burst through the door behind him, Jack realized this is the place where he would probably die.

Sal lunged at Jack, but Jack was ready. Jack jerked backward, jackhammering his arm into Sal's hand. This broke Sal's grip on his gun. The gun flew off the roof and tumbled six stories to the ground.

Jack jumped on Sal and started pounding his fist into Sal's face. Sal countered with a crippling blow to Jack's gut that sent him crashing against the bell.

Jack fought to remain conscious as Sal

yanked him against the bronze arm of one of the statues. Sal jackhammered two more blows into Jack's chest then clamped his huge hands around Jack's neck.

Jack gasped for breath as Sal started choking the life from him. Jack was helpless under his grip.

On the clock above them, the minute hand was about to touch *twelve* as the second hand swept around the clock's face.

Beneath it, Jack kicked at Sal in vain, as Jack's face turned blue, saliva oozing from his mouth.

On the clock's face, the second hand closed in on twelve as, beneath it, Jack's body finally went limp.

As the last breath was about to leave Jack's body, Sal's fingers started to whiten from the pressure of his deadly grip around Jack's neck.

CLICK. The second and the minute hand *both reached twelve* above them. Sal was momentarily distracted by the shifting of the large iron gears inside the clock.

One of the statue's massive bronze arms swung back into position to strike the bell.

The knight's arm ratcheted backward and smashed into Sal and Jack. It knocked them both off the platform.

Sal's body *crashed* through the railing and flipped over the side!

Jack had managed to grab hold of the railing and was dangling over the side. Sal tried to hold onto Jack, but Sal's hands were so weak from applying pressure to Jack's throat that he lost his grip. Sal eyed Jack terrified as his hands slipped from Jack's leg and he tumbled downwards, flailing in the morning air.

Jack gulped air frantically as he watched Sal's body sail down the side of the bell tower, plunging six stories before it finally landed on the granite stones paving the Piazza San Marco below. Jack forced himself back up onto the granite terrace beneath the bell tower, struggling to catch his breath.

MOMENTS LATER, Sal's lifeless body was surrounded by fluttering pigeons and screaming tourists. Carabinieri whistles blew in the background as perhaps a thousand onlookers crowded in for a look.

Another person watched with keen interest from a few hundred yards away. The *masked Assassin* was hiding now on the balcony of St. Marks watching the carabinieri as they removed Sal's body from the Piazza.

In the distance, Jack slipped unnoticed

down the crowded calle behind the bell tower. More carabinieri were approaching from the Fondamenta. Jack avoided them by ducking into an even narrower calle where he spotted carnival outfits for sale on a mobile display case. While the vendor's back was turned, Jack lifted an outfit and slipped away. He pulled the carnival mask over his face, furled the cape over his back, and then he quickly melted unrecognized into the crowd.

Chapter XVIII

Giorgio shut the door to his office, determined to hide the mushrooming scandal from his assistants who were working outside in the Accademia's galleries. His voice was hoarse. He'd been on the phone twenty minutes arguing with Jack and the thought of the carabinieri's investigation reaching his desk was more than he could bear. Because of Jack's absurd ramblings, Giorgio was now defending Carlo Bellini's mistress, a woman he barely knew. Giorgio *had* met Franchesca in the past. She was beautiful, a tempting mistress for anyone that could have her (and many did), but she was certainly *not*, as Jack proposed, a cold-blooded killer. If she were, she would have to be killing *in absentia* as Giorgio was trying to explain to Jack over the phone.

"I'm telling you Franchesca left the country infuriated after Claudia's suicide note revealed Carlo's involvement with other women. It's preposterous she could be behind all this,"

Giorgio claimed emphatically. "The woman *is not* in Italy."

Jack was a few meters away on his cellphone hidden in an alcove beneath the Accademia. He was still wearing the carnival mask and it muffled Jack's frustration. "I don't have time to argue with you, Giorgio!" Jack yelled back into his cellphone. "I'm telling you it's *Franchesca!* She's framed me, and I got every cop in Venice on my ass! Now, are you gonna help me or what?"

Giorgio took a few moments to answer. When he did, he immediately regretted it. "All right," he said reluctantly. "What can I do?"

"Call your contacts at Bellini's law firm and find out about Bellini's will," Jack instructed, flipping up his mask so he could breathe more easily. "Claudia told me Carlo was going to cut Franchesca in on it. If he did, that's motive. Franchesca's share would get bigger with Claudia's death, even bigger with the death of his partners."

"But Franchesca is just a model, for God's sake! She's just a girl!"

"How many murder cases have you worked, Giorgio?" There was silence after that. Jack broke it. "That's what I thought. See, I've worked over fifty. And when I was green, each time the verdict came down, and the guilty did their perp walk out of the courtroom, I'd say to myself—*Wow, he was just a pizza deliveryman, she was just a housewife, what the fuck, how could they do that?* Then I realized it's in *all* of us. We just gotta have enough motive. What's Transitalia worth, Giorgio?"

"I don't know the exact amount but certainly billions of euros."

"Billions with an *'s'?*"

"Yes, *billions*."

"Now that's motive, Giorgio. Motive enough for a *model*, motive enough for anyone. Just go with me on this. *Find out* about Bellini's will."

"Okay," Giorgio finally answered, starting to come around. "How will I find you?"

"Meet me at the Palazzo Gussoni in an hour." Then a realization swept over him, one he grappled with aloud to Giorgio. "Christ, I don't even know who I'm up against... I don't even know what she looks like."

"I've only met Franchesca once," Giorgio revealed. "She never works in Italy. She only models in France."

"C'mon, Giorgio," Jack pressed. "You can do better. There must be something?"

Giorgio thought about it a few seconds then

it finally hit him. "Franchesca made quite a splash last year at a fashion show on Bastille Day in Paris. She wore a mermaid's costume. You may not find it on the net, but one of the local papers here would have covered it. They still store hard copies the old fashioned way in the stacks of St. Mark's."

"Perfect. Thanks, Giorgio. See you in an hour," Jack clicked off quickly. Pulling back down his mask, he rushed off toward the Piazza San Marco.

He was oblivious to someone passing by who was watching him intently—the *chambermaid* from the Palazzo Giovanni.

THE READING ROOM in the Library of Saint Mark was rarely frequented by the casual tourist. Its massive baroque ceilings held up by elaborate stone arches made the centerpiece of the library into a cathedral-like sanctuary. In all of Jack's visits to Venice, and they had been plentiful, the library was never part of his itinerary. But it was today.

Still dressed in his carnival costume, Jack crossed the long narrow floor of the sky-lit reading room toward the research desk. No one seemed to mind. Jack scanned the area for television monitors to make sure his face with a *suspect* label was not gracing their screens. No TVs were present in the library. The establishment was old school, solemn and musty, complete with a matching matronly librarian who Jack approached removing his mask as a courtesy.

"I need something researched," Jack asked the elderly Librarian, in a bit of a rush.

"We don't *research* anything anymore, signor," the librarian answered dismissively without looking up at him. "You must do it yourself." She pointed to a large room off to the side of the library. "The stacks and computers are there."

Government bureaucrats were probably highest on the list of people Jack despised, but lifelong civil servants certainly ran a close second. Jack tried to be civil but failed at it immediately, his words knifing bluntly into the cloud of stillness the librarian was intent on defending. "Listen, *Miss*, I'm in a hurry. If you just …"

The librarian finally locked eyes with him wearing a gin-upped smile that was less convincing than the one on Jack's mask. "It's against policy, signor."

"Look, *Signora*, a friend of mine was here yesterday, and the librarian was very cooperative. He researched something for her and sent it over to our hotel," Jack explained impatiently.

"That's impossible. I'm the only one in this department."

Jack was getting nervous now, certain she was making a mistake—and terrified maybe she wasn't. "You must have seen her. She's American," he pressed, gesturing, "about this tall. Very pretty."

The librarian had enough. "*No* American used our research facilities yesterday and *no* research was sent out."

Jack just stared at her stunned for a moment, deciding to do the calculus on that revelation later. For now, he would stick to the matter at hand. He softened both his tone and his approach. "The fashion show on Bastille Day in Paris last year... What local paper covers that sort of thing?"

The librarian answered politely, anxious to get rid of him. "Il Gazzettino. The stacks on the left. Bastille Day is—"

"—July 14, I know." Absent a nod goodbye, Jack moved apprehensively toward the stacks alongside the left side of the library.

JACK PASSED ROW UPON ROW of

newspapers and magazines, stacked neatly on wooden shelves. The internet had its place in Venetian life, but like her preference for paintings over digital snapshots, Venice was keen to hold onto the relics of her past. There were periodicals in the stacks dating back two hundred years. Jack was only interested in one from nine months ago. He brushed past an old woman perusing the archives of Il Gazzettino as he searched for the pile labeled *Iuglio*.

Jack picked up the whole stack and carried it to a reading table. He quickly leafed through them and found the one he was looking for—an Il Gazzettino daily, labeled *'Iuglio quindicesimo'* July 15th. The day *after* Bastille Day.

He hurriedly flipped pages to find the fashion section. There. Finally. Shots of models prancing down runways in Paris. Jack stared at them frustrated. Beautiful women all, but no mermaids.

Jack turned the page impatiently. There. Jack finally hit pay dirt—a photo of a young model in a *mermaid's costume.* Her body was outrageous. Jack stared at her, his heart stopping, his eyes widening as he saw her dark eyes and short dark hair that partially obscured a face that looked incredibly like—

AMANDA!

Jack's jaw dropped. His heart began racing as he strained to breathe.

"That fucking bitch!" he yelled unattenuated.

The old woman glared at him. Jack didn't care. He grabbed the newspaper and moved across the reading room floor toward an alcove. An armed security guard watched him closely, having heard his outburst.

Huddled under an alcove for privacy, Jack started to dial a number on his cellphone. Then he stopped, struggling to regain his composure. He recovered, and then dialed the international operator.

"Yes, I need directory assistance for Syracuse, New York, please. The number of the Syracuse Herald," Jack asked, fighting to stay calm.

He fished out a tiny notepad from his pocket and scribbled it down when the operator provided the number. He clicked off. Then he hurriedly input the digits into his phone and waited for an answer.

He heard two rings. Finally, a perky receptionist's voice squeaked in his earpiece "Good morning, Syracuse Herald."

"Ah, hi," Jack replied. "I'm calling internationally. Do you have an *Amanda Parks* working there? I believe she writes a gossip column for you?"

"As a matter of fact, we do, sir," the receptionist replied. "But I believe she's on vacation. Please hold on a second."

The receptionist put him on hold before Jack could interrupt. He hung there thoroughly confused, trying to put it all together as the receptionist finally came back on the line.

"She's still on vacation, sir. Can I take a message for her?"

"Do you happen to know where?" Jack said firmly. "It's *extremely* important."

"I believe she went to Miami, sir. She goes there often—to visit her grandchildren."

Grandchildren! Jesus! he thought. Devastated, Jack hung up. His stomach was in knots. His worst fears were confirmed. He beat his hands against the wall, pissed he'd been such a patsy. Franchesca had been *masquerading* as a reporter. She probably grabbed Amanda's name from a copy of the Herald she came across in an airport somewhere. *But why?* he thought. *Why did she return to the scene of Claudia's murder? Why was she manipulating him?* Those answers would have to wait.

Jack got up quickly seeing the security guard moving toward him. The old woman had complained about his conduct, specifically his foul language.

Jack quickly slipped his mask back on and started walking out. The security guard followed him.

Jack picked up his pace trying to get out the door. The security guard caught up with him and blocked his path.

"You can't, signor," the guard said firmly.

Jack's breathing quickened. Everybody was staring at him. He spotted two carabinieri outside. He wanted to make a run for it. He tried to move past the guard. But the guard didn't budge.

"You can't do that, signor," repeated the guard.

"What's the problem?" Jack asked unnerved. "I'm just trying to leave!"

Jack was losing it. The guard shook his head and pointed to the copy of Il Gazzettino that Jack was holding in his hand.

"You cannot take. Capisce?" the guard said impatiently.

Jack finally figured it out. He smiled nervously and handed the newspaper over to the guard.

"Scusate," Jack said relieved.

The guard nodded and opened the door, which Jack exited appreciatively. Protected by the anonymity of his costume, Jack passed the two carabinieri outside and slipped away into the crowd.

Chapter XIX

Giorgio hovered above Jack, who sat in a sea of confusion under stone relics lining a small, walled campi.

"I should've figured it out the moment she showed up," Jack lamented, recounting his first memory of Amanda/Franchesca's arrival. "The moment she made a beeline for the bathroom."

Jack played back the images, over and over again, in his mind—

Franchesca posing as 'Amanda' insisting on using the bathroom, rushing past him inside Room 502 and locking the bathroom door be-hind her.

It seemed obvious now what she was up to. *How could he have been so stupid?* he thought to himself.

"She was looking for the *ring*," Jack continued. "She must've figured it had fallen off in the tub where she was soaking Claudia's body with the grappa after she killed her. She worked me like a fucking puppet, Giorgio!"

"But *why*?" asked Giorgio, still unconvinced. "What would Franchesca, Amanda, or whatever she's calling herself, what would she have to *gain* from the murders?"

"You tell me. The answer has to be in Carlo's will. What did you find out from Bellini's attorneys?"

"That Carlo is beside himself," Giorgio answered. "Claudia's shares were always supposed to revert back to him in the event of her death. But last month, Claudia changed her beneficiary to some friend of hers, an old woman in Rome. Carlo has lost *half* his stake in Transitalia."

"It serves the bastard right. What about Franchesca?"

"This is where it doesn't add up. Apparently, Carlo *had* planned to name Franchesca as his beneficiary after the next board meeting. But Claudia's suicide, or murder, changed his mind. Carlo's lawyers still maintain that Franchesca broke up with Carlo after Claudia's death. She didn't even do it in person. Supposedly, she just sent him a letter saying it was over and then she left the country. So you see, Jack, Franchesca was never even named in the will. Franchesca ended up with *nothing*."

Jack stood up and started pacing, his mind

grappling for an answer.

"Then maybe Franchesca's knocking them all off for revenge?" Jack deduced. "She's slept with everyone in town, for chrissakes. They probably all promised her a piece of the action, and then snubbed her, just like Carlo did with his will."

"Then why is Carlo still alive?" Giorgio asked.

"Because Carlo's the most protected," Jack replied. Then it finally hit him. "Or because he's *next*."

Consumed by his theory, Jack started walking away.

"Where are you going?" Giorgio called out after him.

"To prove it," Jack yelled back without turning.

"But you're a wanted man, Jack!" Giorgio warned. "The carabinieri—"

Jack slipped his mask back down and pointed at it as he turned back briefly to Giorgio. The costume he *appropriated* was generic. There were hundreds like it moving around Venice during the Carnivale. Jack was safe. For now.

Giorgio watched Jack slip into a crowded calle and disappear into a flood of tourists.

AN HOUR LATER, Jack was standing in the shadows on the perimeter of a small campi across from the side entrance of the Palazzo Giovanni. Two carabinieri were in the hotel's lobby. They didn't notice Jack and, even if they had, his identity remained invisible. Jack alerted to someone exiting a side door of the hotel. It was the person he'd been waiting for—the *chambermaid*.

She was heading in Jack's direction. Jack stepped back unnoticed. A few seconds after she had passed him, Jack started to follow.

The chambermaid wound through one calle and into another. She was weaving expertly through the serpentine passages like a typical Venetian. A tourist would have taken three times longer to get where she was going, no doubt getting lost along the way.

She cut through an alcove and traversed a small bridge. Jack kept shadowing her. He didn't care where she was going; he was just waiting for the chance to confront her without witnesses before she got there.

Jack got his chance. She took a shortcut through an empty courtyard. Jack put himself in her path. When he passed her, he shifted and stopped inches in front of her. He slipped off his mask. She gasped. It startled her, which was the intended effect.

"Make it easy for yourself," Jack demanded. "I just want information."

It looked like she was about to scream. Before she could, Jack clamped his hand down on her mouth. She was terrified, and Jack was okay with that.

"Look, I don't want to hurt you," he said firmly. "But if you scream, I'll break your neck. Capisce?"

She nodded, deathly afraid of him. He eased off and began to question her.

"The woman staying with me? Did she pay you to sleep with me?"

The chambermaid shook her head *no* then she turned away from Jack in shame. She was fighting not to cry. She looked like an innocent. Jack felt like shit. He switched gears.

"It's okay, it's okay. You're not in trouble. I just want the truth. What about the magazines and newspapers? Who brought them to the hotel?"

"She did," the chambermaid replied, her voice trembling. "She asked me to bring them to your room."

Jack soaked it all in. "Where is she now?"

"I do not know, signor. Honestly, I don't

know. She left the hotel this morning with her luggage."

"For where?!" Jack pressed.

The chambermaid only replied with a shrug. Not the answer Jack was looking for. He shook her angrily. "Come on, you must've seen something! Did she leave in a water taxi for the airport? The train station?"

"I do not know!" the chambermaid pleaded, starting to cry. "I delivered the envelope she was waiting for then she left."

"Envelope? What was in it?" Jack demanded, finally letting her go.

"Tickets maybe," the chambermaid answered, trying to compose herself. "I didn't look inside. It was sent from the Agencie Fenice."

Jack studied her a moment. Her eyes, the part of them he could see through her tears, were sincere. She was just standing there trembling, trying not to break down again. He didn't know how deeply she was involved, but he could tell she had been an unwitting pawn. He dug into his pocket and pulled out some euros. He tried to give them to her. She batted them away angrily.

"I don't want your money," she screamed. "I'm not a whore!"

The chambermaid ran off humiliated leaving Jack remorseful and alone behind her.

BY THE TIME THE SUN started to dip beneath the Veneto, Jack had made his way to the window of the Agencie Fenice, a ticket agency near the recently renovated Teatro Fenice on the Campo San Fantin.

The ticket office was closing in two minutes and the aggravated look on the female agent's face was typical for a Venetian clerk near closing time. Business hours in Venice were *flexible*. And that flexibility never favored the customer. Jack was lucky the clerk found him attractive.

Mask off, Jack was leaning into her window spinning his tale of woe.

"There's been a mix-up. My wife bought two tickets over the phone and only one was delivered to our hotel," Jack told the female clerk."

"For what event, signor?" the ticket agent replied cooperatively.

"Ah, ah…" Jack stumbled. "Well, see it was actually a surprise for our anniversary. So, to be quite honest, she didn't tell me."

The agent stared at him quizzically. Jack smiled sheepishly. She checked her watch.

Anxious to get out of there, she played along. "What's the name, then?" she asked, getting ready to type it into her database.

"Amanda Parks. We're staying at the Hotel Giovanni."

The agent checked her records. She found the entry quickly. Jack perked as she nodded.

"It's here," she said. "One ticket for the Festa di Carnevale. Tonight at the Corderie." Then she scrolled down two fields on her computer screen and frowned. "But it was delivered this morning?"

"Hmmm ..." Jack said, feigning surprise. "Well, we were supposed to get two. I guess I'll just buy another. How much are they?"

"One hundred fifty euros, signor."

Jack nodded and fished out two hundred euros from his pocket. The Agent gave him the extra ticket and his change. Jack nodded a hurried *thanks* then slipped his mask back down and walked away.

"Felice anniversario, signor!" she called out after him.

"What?" said Jack confused as he looked back at her.

"Happy Anniversary!" the Agent replied.

"Oh, right!" Jack said recovering. "Thank you! I'm really looking forward to it!"

For Jack, no words were ever truer. Jack slipped back into the crowd, nervously watching for the carabinieri.

THE CORDERIE WAS MASSIVE. Towering vaulted ceilings and a stadium-length hall with a capacity to hold over two thousand guests. Built in the fourteenth century, the Corderie was designed to manufacture ropes for the rigging of the ships that Venice built for herself and her customers. For the last fifty years, it had been repurposed for various festivities and lent itself handily to the debauchery of the all-night raves prevalent during the Carnevale. It was located at the edge of the Arsenale and surrounded by fortress-like walls. Bulletproof security was its most desirable feature, the visiting royals and elite preferring the venue for this reason. They partied harder knowing their orgiastic feasts would not be witnessed by anyone other than their peers.

Tonight, the bass from the music blaring inside the Corderie could be heard miles away from the Arsenale. Jack pushed through the mob waiting at the Corderie's entrance, still concealed beneath his cape and mask.

He showed his ticket to a costumed bouncer outside and waded through the chaos as a D.J.

on stage mixed up a heart-pounding set of vintage trance/electronica that whipped the crowd into a frenzy.

Once inside, Jack scanned the thousand bodies writhing on the dance floor. The music was unbearably loud. Jack had to fight his way through gyrating, colliding bodies to reach the center of the crowd where he spotted a dancer wearing the same mask as the assassin who killed Torelli at the Ducale.

As he homed in on the dancer, he saw female legs poke out from under the costume. He was sure it must be Amanda/Franchesca—or whatever her real name was. At this point, Jack didn't care. He just needed to confront her and have her arrested. Then all the madness would end.

Jack cut in on the dancer's partner. The partner was so drunk he didn't notice. The dancer didn't mind either. She continued dancing with Jack, who moved forward abruptly and whipped the mask off her face.

Jack frowned. The dancer's face was even more hideous than her mask. And it definitely wasn't the one he was looking for. The outraged carnival goer glared at him as Jack slipped back into the crowd.

Jack scanned the dance floor frantically.

There. Another one. Same mask, similar cape. Jack stalked her on the dance floor as she gyrated. When he caught up to her, she turned and began dancing seductively, shaking her hips. Hips wider than the Grand Canal. Even Jack's mask frowned and he moved on.

Jack pulled up his mask and stared hopelessly into the throng. Finding his target was impossible. The D.J. triggered a new, heart-throbbing beat, which hypnotically convulsed the crowd.

Jack's breathing stopped as he caught sight of a familiar mask on someone dancing twenty yards away from him. It was the *triple-faced mask* that Amanda had shown him inside Room 502.

Jack slid down his mask and crossed over to her. Gold sequin straps were the only thing covering the dancer's sensual body, the rest of it covered by a transparent silk mesh. Her breasts were heaving to the beat. As Jack drew near, he got the confirmation he'd been waiting for—the dancer in the triple-face mask was wearing a *black cameo* on her neck—the same one Amanda wore when she was naked in the fountain in the Villa Eden.

Jack slid up next to her. She launched into a serpentine grind so erotic the other dancers stopped to watch. Her body pumped seductive-ly. Still hidden by his mask, Jack started danc-ing with her. She welcomed it. The music got louder as the two of them danced a few sec-onds before Jack motioned her over to the side.

He danced, moving backward. She fol-lowed, undulating to the beat. They were off to the side now alone, dancing inches from each other. Then Jack made his move. He ripped the mask from her face. He was right. He stared at her angrily. Amanda stared back at him in shock—

"Jack??" she said recovering.

Jack waved a finger at her furiously. "Don't! Don't make it worse!"

She looked at him confused a second, then faked concern. "I feel so bad for you, Jack. They want you for murder—"

Jack lost it. He grabbed her. Shoved her against a wall. "No more bullshit! *Do You Hear Me!*

"You're hurting me!" she groaned.

"You're lucky I don't rip your heart out!" Jack said angrily, easing his grip. "*Why me*, Amanda? Or Franchesca, or whatever the hell your name is? WHY ME!!"

"Because you were there, Jack!" she an-swered venomously, struggling to get out of his grip. "You were easy. And you were a great *fuck*. That one, I didn't expect." Then she looked at him almost genuinely for a moment, her eyes seemingly filled with regret.

Jack didn't notice. He was too overcome with confusion and rage. "How could you do it?" he said bitterly. *"HOW COULD YOU?"*

Amanda stared at the floor zombie-like, thrown as if confronting him made her face something inside herself. This was uncharted territory for the callous, unfeeling sociopath she had become. She finally looked up at him, almost somnambulate, confused.

"It doesn't have to end like this, Jack," she mumbled as if thinking out loud. "Maybe we can have something, you and me ... Maybe we can ..."

Jack glared at her, incredulous. "You and *me*? What could I possibly want with *you*? You repulse me!" He grabbed her again, shaking her angrily. "What am I supposed to do now? Help you with the next one on your list? Help you kill *Carlo!"*

Amanda pulled away. His words had cut deep. He had dismissed her overture callously and reminded her of everything she had learned to hate in men. The venom welled back up inside her. She glared at him with an unnerving calm

"You're a bigger fool than I thought, Jack," she gloated. "I *love* Carlo. Who do you think I'm doing this for?"

Jack was stunned. He eased up on his grip as she smiled icily, staring at something behind him.

"You really wanna know who's next, Jack?" she taunted. *"You are!"*

Jack spun around to see what she was looking at. Across the dance floor, a squad of carabinieri were racing toward him. The *chambermaid* was trailing behind them, pointing the way.

Jack turned crazed toward Amanda whereupon she unleashed a *deafening scream*. The music stopped. All eyes turned to Jack. The carabinieri's whistles blew and they closed in.

Jack freaked. He bolted frantically into the crowd, knocking away everyone in his path.

The carabinieri were tight on his heels. Jack barreled through a side door and charged out into a corridor.

The carabinieri were just yards behind him. He reached the end of the corridor and bounded down a staircase.

The carabinieri followed. Three floors below, they finally reached the base of the stairs. Jack was nowhere to be found. One of the carabinieri pointed to a door at the edge of the hallway. The carabinieri raced over to it and charged outside.

Seconds later, at the base of the stairway, Jack dropped down from the crevice beneath the stairs where he had been hiding. He listened for any sign of the carabinieri. Silence. He was free. For now. He raced back up the stairs to the landing on the floor above him.

He slipped out the window to the metal fire escape outside and climbed down to the safety of the darkness below.

Chapter XX

Jack was a beaten man. Every molecule in his body ached, especially the ones in his heart. He was hiding in the shadows of an alcove off the Fondamenta. Cell phone to his ear, he waited impatiently for someone to answer. Three rings, four rings, finally…

"Hello?" his estranged wife said groggily on the other end of the line.

Jack waited a long beat before answering. Dialing Kate at a time like this was one thing. Actually talking to her, admitting to his dire circumstance was another. He settled for something in between.

"Hi," Jack said tentatively. "Please don't hang up."

Kate was surprised to hear his voice. She was silent a moment before the bitterness activated her vocal chords.

"What's the matter, Jack?" she finally snapped. "Your little tramp in the hotel finally get bored with you?"

"Kate, stop," Jack said weakly, into his cell phone. "I didn't call to argue."

"Then why did you call, Jack?"

Jack was silent a moment. "I don't know, really… just to hear your voice," he finally muttered, almost to himself.

"Well, you're hearing my goddamn voice, Jack! And so will your attorney when I tell him I'm taking everything you've got!"

Jack was too shaken to fight back. "Yeah— well, I miss you too, Kate."

There was a long beat of silence. Kate got nervous. She knew he wasn't himself. They had ten years. Some of the good memories flooded into the well of pain inside her. She softened her tone. "What's wrong with you Jack? You don't sound too good."

Jack realized the answer to that question would take hours, perhaps even years. So he decided just to hang up. But before he did, he gave her something, a confession perhaps, a couple of sentences on the fly. And after uttering them, he realized they were sufficient.

"I just wanted to tell you that you were right, Kate. You were right about the grass," Jack admitted. "It sure as hell ain't greener."

"Jack? You're freaking me out," Kate replied. "What is *wrong* with you?"

Click. Jack had already hung up, over-whelmed by the relentless anguish in his gut. Suddenly, he caught sight of a woman walking across the docks. She was heading for the motoscafos waiting on the Fondamenta about a hundred yards from him.

It was *Amanda*.

She was alone. She climbed into a private water taxi. Jack quickly dialed another number on his cell phone. A carabiniere answered.

"Get me Captain Giovanni," Jack said urgently. "Tell him it's Jack Sands."

As he waited for Lucca to come on the line, Jack watched Amanda's motoscafo head away from Venice toward the islands beyond in the lagoon. Lucca finally answered.

"Running will only make things worse, Jack," Lucca warned from behind his desk.

"I come in my own way, Lucca. That's how it's gotta be."

"I'm listening," Lucca replied, playing along.

"One hour. Top of the Rialto. Come alone. I'll be unarmed."

"You're not in a position to dictate terms, Jack!" Lucca snapped irritated.

"You want me the easy way, Lucca? Or you wanna search every rotten canal in Venice to find me?"

Lucca stared at Rizzo. Rizzo was standing next to three other carabinieri in his office, all chomping at the bit to take down Jack. Lucca calmed and turned back to the phone. "One hour. Top of the Rialto," Lucca replied. *"Don't fuck me, Jack."*

Jack's response was dial tone. He shoved his phone in his pocket and raced down toward the docks in the distance.

JACK REACHED THE MOTOSCAFO STAND barely a minute after Amanda had departed. There was only one water taxi remaining. Jack anxiously flagged the driver and climbed on the boat.

"Take me to the Isola San Lazzaro," Jack instructed, pointing in the direction Amanda had gone.

"The island is a private residence, signor," the driver responded. "Are you a friend of the Bellinis?"

Jack pulled out two hundred euros. "Yeah. A good friend," Jack replied, flashing the euros in front of him. "And if you get me there quick, I'll be a good friend of yours."

The driver nodded. It was two in the morning. Chances of finding another fare at this hour were slim. Finding one that tipped as handsomely, even slimmer. The driver revved the engine and the motoscafo knifed into the icy waters of the lagoon.

The tiny island of San Lazzaro lay between Venice and the Lido. Starting its life as one of the many muddy outcrops of the Veneto, a fortress-like structure was built there to house lepers in the seventeenth century. Its walls were high, the lepers believing their design was to keep people out. Eventually, they discovered the walls were built to keep them in. As the lepers died off or were forced to rot on less *expensive* real estate, San Lazzaro became home to a Catholic Monastery.

Until the twentieth century, Catholic tithings managed to fund operations for the monks cloistered there. But twenty-one hundred years after the death of the Church's patriarch, Catholicism fell out of favor with the masses, especially the wealthier among them and the funds dried up.

In search of a new benefactor, the monks found one in Carlo Bellini. Carlo was in search of privacy and privacy was impossible to find in Venice. He committed to investing a small fortune in the monastery in return for permission to convert an old armory on the edge of the island into a private residence. It was the first of its kind on San Lazzaro, and because of the public outrage the deal incurred, it was destined to be its last. Carlo spent millions on the place and made sure it was guarded accordingly.

Jack had always wanted to get a look at it. Tonight he would get his chance. Franchesca, Amanda, whatever she was calling herself, was obviously heading there to reunite with Carlo. They had orchestrated their twisted scheme perfectly. Jack remained its only loose end. And Jack was determined to keep it that way. His motoscafo bounced hard on the choppy waters of the lagoon, which were black as coal until—

A *white searchlight* blinded Jack from another boat approaching fast from the west. The driver slowed.

"It's the carabinieri, signor," the driver said nervously.

"Don't stop!" Jack commanded firmly.

The driver ignored him and started to kill the engine. Jack angrily grabbed the wheel. The carabinieri closed in, their sirens blaring as they saw Jack's motoscafo turn away.

The driver shouted angrily at Jack in Italian while struggling to get control of the vessel.

Aiming their spotlight on the water taxi, the carabinieri roaring toward them watched Jack fight with the driver. The driver was pounding on Jack's back viciously trying to break his grip on the wheel. Jack finally had enough and slammed his elbow into the driver's face jettisoning him into the water.

Motoscafos are actually relatively high-performance vessels, performing better the lighter the load. And the proof of this was the uncanny speed the motoscafo attained after Jack floored the vessel now that it was absent its captain.

The water taxi quickly distanced itself from the carabinieri's pursuit, turning away from the island and making a beeline for the safety of the Lido.

The carabinieri were pissed and relentless. They ignored the waving driver bobbing in the water helplessly as they sped off after Jack. One of the carabinieri barked into a walkie-talkie for backup as he sent up a flare. The foggy skies above the lagoon filled with a fiery crimson light.

The carabinieri boat was running wide open. The roar of its dual diesel motors was menacing, and Jack could hear it from a mile away as he pounded through the half-meter waves lapping on the edge of the Lido.

As he neared the docks on the Lido's beach,   another police boat appeared on the horizon. Both boats vectored in on him as a carabinieri squad car stopped on the dock ahead.

Jack was out of moves. He eyed the beach a hundred yards from the dock and buried the throttle. The motoscafo rocketed toward it.

Reaching the beach in less than five seconds, Jack's water taxi pounded into the sand, its hull burrowing and slamming it to a stop.

Jack jumped off his motoscafo as the carabinieri boats hovered off shore, trailing his escape with spotlights.

On the narrow road circling the perimeter of the Lido, two carabinieri squad cars barreled toward Jack as he raced toward a Fiat taxi parked under a street lamp.

The taxi driver barely had time to react, let alone protest, as Jack pulled him out of the car, threw a wad of euros at him, and jumped inside, slamming the door and grabbing the wheel. The driver watched incredulously as Jack sped away—until he eyed the euros in his hand. There must have been three hundred of them. Jack was down almost seven hundred for the night if you counted the ticket to the Corderie. But the way he drove like a maniac through the streets of the Lido, suggested he wasn't counting. Jack only had two things on his mind. First, surviving. Second, getting even with Carlo and his girlfriend.

The survival part might be tricky. The Lido's roads were treacherously narrow. Especially when traveling at 110 kilometers an hour with two squad cars in pursuit.

The chase heated up quickly. Jack floored the Fiat down the sliver of highway that wove through the spine of the Lido.

The two carabinieri squad cars closed in behind him as Jack hung a sharp left down a side street. Bad move. Two more carabinieri squad cars whipped around a corner and barreled toward him, head on. Their flashing lights blinding his eyes, Jack jerked the Fiat's wheel hard right.

The Fiat skidded around a corner onto a one-way street. Of course, the Fiat was traveling the wrong direction, but since it was now racing along at 120 kilometers per hour, it would probably pass by before anyone had the chance to care.

All four carabinieri squad cars roared onto the street behind him. Jack gunned the engine. The eighty horsepower four-banger didn't have much left, but he got another ten kilometers per hour out of it. And it groaned in protest accordingly, almost sensing the menace ahead, which its high beams illuminated fifty yards in the distance.

Jack's eyes opened wide eyeing a *gelato cart* parked sideways on the road. Jack pounded on his horn, screaming at the elderly couple pushing the cart.

The old couple waved frantically, screaming in Italian for Jack to stop.

But Jack couldn't stop; the carabinieri were right on his ass. One of the cops leaned out a window and fired an Uzi blowing out Jack's rear windshield as Jack barreled toward the cart.

The old couple freaked and used all their strength to try to push the car out of the way. Jack freaked himself, finally understanding the reason they were waving and screaming at him to stop. It wasn't because they feared he would run into their cart. It was because beyond the cart, in the space of fewer than five meters, the road Jack was traveling *dead-ended* into the lagoon!

Jack first became aware of that fact as the couple managed to push the cart out of his way. Jack's reflexes were quick. It was probably less than ten milliseconds before his foot jerked off the accelerator and slammed down on the brake. But at 130 kilometers per hour, even one millisecond wouldn't have been fast enough.

The old couple screamed as Jack's Fiat crashed through a wooden barrier, sailed fifty feet through the air and was swallowed up by the choppy waters of the icy lagoon.

Chapter XXI

The carabinieri boats circled the murky depths. Their spotlights illuminated the water for the divers searching for Jack's submerged Fiat. A carabiniere radioed his superior.

Lucca got the call while waiting impatiently three miles away on top of the Rialto Bridge with his men. Jack had double-crossed him, this much he knew, but until they found Jack's body—dead, drowned, or otherwise, the case was still open. This did not sit well with Lucca. He would have preferred a rough interrogation followed by a full confession, at minimum the suspect's corpse, but Jack had denied him any of that. He motioned to Rizzo, and they rushed off to a boat waiting for them underneath the Rialto.

THE WATER OFF ISOLA SAN LAZZARO was ten degrees colder than the water circling Venice herself. No one really knew the reason. Sure, there was speculation, scientific studies of tidal currents, even some mention of mineral content from the quarried rocks undergirding its foundation. But legend had it that an ancient spell accounted for the discrepancy.

Many lepers had died there. One was burned in his youth for the crime of sorcery. As he died, the legend maintained, the boy cast a spell on the water ensuring its temperature stayed cold enough to trigger hypothermia for anyone choosing to swim there. Three soldiers guarding the leper colony became the spell's first victims. They died from the cold and the currents while swimming recreationally. And six hundred years later, as a result of the spell, the minerals, the currents, or whatever, the cold remained.

And one man was a reluctant witness to it. As hypothermia was about to take him, Jack flailed in the icy water struggling to reach shore.

Swimming the last three feet to safety, Jack clung to the wall rising up on the edge of the Isola San Lazzaro. He shivered like a drowned rat. Under cover of darkness, he forced himself onto the rocky shore on the perimeter of Carlo Bellini's palatial estate.

Jack slithered across the grass on his stomach, keeping an eye on an armed guard patrolling the grounds.

Still struggling to breathe normally, he crawled toward Bellini's mansion. He spotted Carlo himself in a third story window. Carlo was looking out over the lagoon toward the divers and carabinieri boats off the Lido. Carlo watched the commotion as a spectator, never thinking for a second it related to him or the night that would change his life forever.

Jack made his way to a window on the first floor. He peered through the glass looking for a way inside.

Jack jumped back suddenly as a *huge Great Dane* lunged at the window, barking viciously from inside the house. Jack's heart raced. A light danced on the back of his head. Jack spun, finding a flashlight glaring in his eyes.

He finally regained focus and saw that the light was held by Bellini's *skyscraper bodyguard.* He had seen the skyscraper previously the night he first met the trio of partners at the Giovanni. Jack started to speak, but a hard right to Jack's mouth from the bodyguard interrupted Jack's oratory. Jack crashed to the ground unconscious.

MINUTES LATER, Jack shivered with a badly swollen jaw leaning against the balustrade of a large octagonal terrace at the edge of the Isola San Lazzaro. The lights from the Piazza San Marco twinkled in the background as Carlo Bellini approached from the mansion.

The Skyscraper and another guard holding the Great Dane both covered Jack from a distance at the base of the steps to the terrace. Bellini wanted to confront Jack privately. In addition to his wrath, Jack had earned Bellini's curiosity.

Bellini climbed up the steps of the octagonal terrace. It was one of his favorite places on the island, a spot favored by the Catholic monks of old for its breathtaking view of Venice. But tonight, Bellini wasn't looking at the view. He was looking at the man eyeing him venomously from the edge of the balustrade.

"The carabinieri are on their way," Bellini said with a thin smile as he moved in closer to Jack. He proceeded to slap Jack angrily with the back of his hand. Jack started to lunge at him but stopped hearing the guard at the base of the steps ratchet the chamber of his shotgun.

"Go ahead, touch me," Bellini said icily. "Give my men an excuse."

Jack backed off.

Bellini stared at Jack disgusted a moment and then got right in his face.

"Why did you do it?" Carlo said bitterly. "Revenge? Was my wife so seductive that her death drove you to this madness? What kind of sick human being are you?"

Jack glared back at him, equally disgusted. "Cut the bullshit, Carlo. It's just you and me." Jack searched the grounds with his eyes then turned back to Carlo. "Where's Franchesca? At least have her show herself, play out the rest of the charade in front of Lucca," Jack taunted. "I'd like to see *that* performance. She's very good at what she does."

Carlo stared at him blankly. "I haven't seen Franchesca since Claudia committed suicide."

"Of course, you haven't seen her," Jack said cynically, "because you sent her to the room for the ring she left behind after murdering your wife!"

"You're insane. A maniac. You're truly deranged."

"Am I?" replied Jack, brazenly moving closer to Bellini. "Who killed Donato? Who shot Torelli? Did your goons do it for you or did Franchesca do it herself?"

Bellini was so surprised by the lunacy of Jack's allegations that he just started laughing.

"Franchesca could never hurt *anybody*," Carlo said firmly. "*Claudia* was the marksman.

201

Franchesca was terrified of guns. She was naïve. She had a mind like a child."

"Oh, come off it, Carlo," Jack said aggravated. "Franchesca or Amanda, whatever that
bitch is calling herself, she's anything but naïve. She's crazy—a goddamn nymph!"

Bellini's face tightened. Jack could see he
was getting to him.

"What a piece of ass, right, Carlo?" Jack
said, continuing to press Bellini. "She was
awesome. The first night she seduced me, she
took me to the Villa Eden—"

Jack paused seeing Carlo's face go pale.

"What's the matter, Carlo?" Jack continued. "She took you there, too? Aw... and I
thought I was *special*. Did she do you in the
fountain? That's where she did me."

That did it. Carlo grabbed Jack and shook
him angrily.

"You're lying!!" Carlo screamed.

Jack smiled, happy his words were cutting
deep.

"Am I, Carlo?" Jack taunted. "Want me to
tell you about the shape of her breasts? About
the mole inside her left thigh?"

Bellini let him go. He was struggling to
breathe.

"You slept with her ..." Bellini said weakly.

"You really slept with her."

"Oh, c'mon, Carlo. *Everybody* did," Jack said callously. "Franchesca was—"

"NO!" Carlo screamed infuriated. "*Claudia! Claudia* was the one who took me to the Villa Eden. *Claudia* had the mole!"

Jack's jaw dropped. His heart pounded as he eyed Carlo incredulously.

"Wait a minute," Jack said, scrambling to understand. "Claudia had blonde hair and blue eyes! I met her, for chrissakes!"

"Claudia was *obsessed* with changing her appearance," Bellini responded emphatically. "She wore contacts. She dyed her hair. Her hair and eyes were *dark,* just like Franchesca's. The two of them could've have been *sisters.*"

Now Jack was the one having trouble breathing. For the next few tortured milliseconds, Jack played back everything in his mind, the images, the memories, the coincidences, the inconsistencies, the incredible, devious brilliance of it all, until he finally blurted out the sick, twisted, incontrovertible epiphany that just detonated in his mind.

"She's still alive…" Jack murmured, almost inaudibly.

"What??" Bellini said confused.

Jack got right in his face.

"Don't you get it yet, Carlo?" Jack said urgently. *"Claudia is still alive!!"*

She certainly was, and she was standing now in the shadows by the door to the boathouse beneath the terrazzo.

Jack only caught sight of her for an instant as she leveled a 9mm handgun in his direction. Jack dove to the ground as *three shots* rang out.

Her strategy, as always, was impeccable. In an instant, the two guards were dead leaving Jack the only one alive. Jack was staring helplessly at Carlo Bellini, who was lying dead beneath him, his temple shattered by a single 9mm bullet.

Jack froze, almost somnambulate, having been caught yet another time in her web. He spotted her heading off silently in a skiff that slipped into the blackness of the lagoon.

Jack got hold of himself and started running toward her, but the Great Dane pounced on him from behind, lunging at his throat. The Dane knocked Jack to the ground, and its jaws started ripping savagely into Jack's chest.

Two shots cracked into the air spooking the dog. Lucca lowered his gun. Lucca, Rizzo, and three other carabinieri ran toward Jack.

They pulled the dog off him. Jack struggled

to stand. He was bleeding badly. The carabinieri checked the other three lifeless bodies as Jack watched Lucca pick up something off the steps.

Lucca held the object up to the light. It was a handgun. A 9mm automatic. Jack stared at it incredulous, eyeing the very familiar *mother of pearl inlays* on its grip as Rizzo handcuffed him and dragged him away.

Chapter XXII

Venetian prisons were notoriously inhospitable. That seemed logical to any Venetian, but to Jack, it came as a bit of a shock. His holding cell was probably built three to four hundred years ago. Its slab granite walls hadn't seen much of a remodel since, and, with the exception of the stainless steel toilet suspended on the wall across from him, a prisoner interred there then probably encountered the same lack of hospitality that Jack was encountering now. But Jack wasn't focused on Venetian hospitality. He was focused like a laser on convincing Lucca of his innocence. Impervious, Lucca listened from the corridor outside the rusted iron bars of Jack's cell.

"You gotta look at motive, Lucca," Jack pleaded. "Mine is too weak."

"On the contrary," Lucca replied impatiently. "Yours is *exceptionally* strong. You met Claudia. You had a brief affair with her. You went back to your home and left your wife for her. You returned to the Giovanni and found her dead. You became enraged, unstable—"

"Goddammit, did you even listen to me, Lucca? I spent two hours with her. I never even *touched* her!"

"Then why did you come back to see her?"

"I don't know... Honestly, I don't," Jack replied as he slumped back down on the bench of his cell. "My marriage was over. I thought maybe we could have something. I was confused."

"Then why were your prints on the gun? The very *same* gun that killed Torelli and Bellini?"

Jack flashed back to Amanda inside Room 502 to the moment when she removed *the silver box with its mother of pearl inlays* from inside her shopping bag. His gut churned as he realized her treachery.

"Because that was the easiest way she could frame me," Jack snapped back. "She took the pearl grips off the gun and glued them to a jewelry box to get my prints. She was a fucking genius, Lucca! She played us all for suckers and she's going to walk if you don't do something!"

"Do what, Jack?" Lucca replied irritated. "The case is open and shut. I've got plenty of evidence to get a conviction."

No one was more aware of that than Jack was. He eyed an Ethiopian street merchant watching them from the cell across the corridor. The Ethiopian was probably being held for illegal vending. *The Ethiopian would be back home in a few days,* Jack thought. He, on the other hand, would be rotting there for life. Capital punishment was banned in Italy shortly after it was conquered by Napoleon. For some, that was a blessing. For Jack, the thought of multiple life sentences served in the putrid bowels of Venice was more than he could bear. He turned back to Lucca, fighting not to unravel.

"Look at me, Lucca. Man to man in my goddamn eyes…"

Lucca stared at Jack a long beat.

"Do you really believe I did it? Do you really believe I'd be stupid enough to kill them all with witnesses breathing down my neck?"

Lucca didn't answer.

Jack glared at him. "Answer me, Lucca!"

Lucca stared at him a moment longer, struggling with the logical inconsistencies of the case.

"I don't know," Lucca finally replied begrudgingly.

Jack perked. Lucca's response was his first microscopic ray of hope.

"Well, can you do me one favor?" Jack pleaded. "My whole goddamn life's on the line here."

Lucca replied reluctantly. "What now, Mr. Sands?"

"Dig up the *body*. Use the DNA lab in Rome for a positive I.D. on the corpse."

"What's that going to prove?"

"That the body *isn't* Claudia."

"Then who the hell is it, Jack?"

Soon, they were going to find out. But it would take a typically foggy Venetian morning and a gravedigger's crew to assist them.

THE CEMETERY on the Isola St. Michelle was an unusually festive place considering the six centuries worth of human remains that populated its soil. Crypts abounded, but simple crosses were more plentiful, all of them dutifully decorated with floral remembrances, both fresh and fake.

As he watched his crew lift Claudia's casket from its freshly dug grave, Lucca couldn't help noticing how beautiful the view of Venice was from the cemetery. The irony that the dead inhabited nicer real estate than a captain in the

Carabinieri was not lost on him.

The crew struggled with the casket. They finally managed to place it on a cart where it would be wheeled to a boat waiting at the entrance on the lagoon. It would have been a simpler matter to remove her body from the casket at its gravesite, saving both time and crew, but Lucca thought the better of it, as his undertaking had already caused quite a stir. The Venetians visiting their fallen loved ones, primarily older women, weren't used to seeing caskets rising *out* of their graves, and Lucca felt adding the spectacle of Claudia's decomposed body to the mix would be too much for them to bear.

Claudia's casket finally reached the boat. It would be on a plane destined for the DNA lab in Rome within the hour.

LATER THAT SAME DAY while Roman technicians in white lab coats examined a sample of Claudia's burnt skin under a high-tech microscope, Jack paced the granite floors of his cell. His Spartan surroundings were without distraction. This, and the knowledge he might be spending the rest of his life there encouraged his mind to focus. His mind complied and his hands assisted by scribbling a jumbled maze of words and phrases on the wall with a stubby piece of chalk he found beneath his cot.

Claudia burned beyond recognition – Amanda arrived the next day – Donato searched for something under the bed – Torelli knew of the passage – Was Rossini in on it?

Jack studied every scratch desperately trying to piece it together. Suddenly, he stopped pacing. Something snapped. He moved quickly to the bars of his cell and yelled at the guard. "I need to use the phone!"

JACK'S REQUEST quickly made its way to Lucca's office. Lucca was buried in paperwork behind his desk when he received it. He had already started feeling sorry for Jack, grappling with the credibility of Jack's guilt himself, so he was predisposed to grant it.

"All right, allow him one call," Lucca said to the guard who waited at the door to his office. The guard nodded and shut the door behind him.

Less than a second later, Rizzo entered from another door on the opposite side of the office. His face was coiled with urgency as he waved at Lucca to follow him down the hall. Lucca complied quickly, presumably knowing the nature of Rizzo's summons.

THE FAX ROOM of carabinieri headquarters was a technological relic, but it was still a bureaucratic mandate in Venice that hardcopy faxes be sent and received to document matters of importance. Emails were swift and expedient but somehow crisp white Venetian paper spitting out of a vintage but well maintained dot-matrix fax machine had a particular captivating verve. Lucca, Rizzo and five others crowded around the relic waiting for the transmission from the DNA lab in Rome.

The first characters to spit onto the page were a stream of unintelligible numbers, presumably internal case IDs, which no one seemed to take note of. The next batch, however, would have more import and Lucca leaned in for a closer look as the letters started tumbling out—

IDENTIFICAZIONE POSITIVO

Positive identity, the characters read. Excellent news, thought Lucca. Whatever the lab found, they found with certainty, which was rare for them as they were in the habit of covering their asses with ambiguity.

As the fax machine's dot-matrix printer head slid into a hard left carriage return, it rotated to punch out the next line.

As it did, everyone in the room leaned forward anxiously. Some even held their breath, knowing these last letters would coalesce into the name that would confirm the identity of the body inside Claudia's casket.

The letters spit out slowly. Times Roman, 14-point, capitalized, double-spaced, and underlined, the name seemed to bang onto the paper with authority. Lucca gasped audibly as he read it—

PANELLI, FRANCHESCA

Chapter XXIII

Lucca waited alone in the carabinieri head-quarters conference room. The fax was in his hand. He couldn't stop staring at it, eyeing Franchesca's name in disbelief. If Franchesca's dead body was the one inside Claudia's casket, then indeed, it was possible, make that proba-ble, Claudia was still alive. But could Claudia be the killer? *Utter madness*, Lucca thought, but he couldn't dismiss the possibility. He just needed someone to walk him through it. Some-one who had spent some time thinking about it. Someone whose life depended on convincing him. And that someone was escorted into the room under carabinieri guard.

Jack could see by the expression on Luc-ca's face that he had been right about Claudia. As Jack entered, Lucca handed him the fax for confirmation. Jack barely read it before explod-ing with vindication and pent up rage.

"What a mind, Lucca! What a woman, what a bitch… what a *conniving bitch!"* Jack announced with a flurry. "Do you believe this, Lucca? We gotta go to *Rome!"*

"What?" Lucca replied, thoroughly confused.

Jack was bouncing off the walls with anticipation. "Rome, Lucca! The answer's in Rome!"

"Would you mind explaining?"

"Do I look like I'd mind explaining? I'm on fire here!" Jack answered with a crazed madness in his eyes.

"Then explain!"

"All right, try and follow me because it's complicated. But it's also genius, and if we fuck around, she's gonna get away with it!"

"I'm listening," Lucca snapped.

"A friend of mine's got the inside line to Bellini's attorneys," Jack explained as he started to circle the conference table. "Claudia planned to fake her death at least a month ago."

"How do you know?"

"Because that's when she *modified* her will by changing her beneficiary from Carlo to someone new. Then she proceeded to kill Carlo before he had a chance to contest and, more importantly, before he could change *his* beneficiary to Franchesca. With Carlo dead and his will unchanged, all of Carlo's shares would have reverted to Claudia. But with Claudia supposedly dead, *both* their shares, that's *thirty-three percent* of Transitalia, the fifth largest shipping company in the world, *all* of those shares now belong to Claudia's beneficiary, some old lady in Rome named Evelyn Manners, someone no one has ever heard of! And it gets better. You wanna hear the rest?"

"Do I have a choice?"

"No," Jack answered, winding himself even tighter. "Look, we know she hated Carlo, right? I heard it from her own mouth the first night I met her, the night she was still Claudia, the night before she staged her own death. But at least Carlo had loved her, he supported her, they must have had something once, yet she had no problem killing him. So the partners, Torelli and Donato, both of whom she des-pised—killing them had to have been easy for her. I mean, you've been in this racket as long as I have, Lucca. Killing gets easier for these animals as the body count rises."

"Go on," Lucca said, nodding reluctantly.

"So with all three partners dead, the other beneficiaries would obviously much rather have three billion dollars cash than the head-ache of running the company, a business they know nothing about, right?"

Lucca nodded again, rubbing the back of his hands impatiently.

"Well, that three billion dollar offer from Bremencorp to buy Transitalia expires at noon tomorrow and Transitalia has convened a special board meeting in Rome to ratify the sale. *That's* where you'll find Evelyn Manners, and I say *that's* where you'll find Claudia Bellini."

Jack slumped exhausted in a chair like a lawyer resting his case.

Lucca hung there a long beat. It was a lot to absorb, but the logic tracked and the clock was ticking.

"And what if you're wrong?" he asked Jack.

"Then you're out a couple of plane tickets. But if I'm right, and we don't get down there—Claudia walks with a *billion* dollars!"

IT WASN'T NORMAL for a murder suspect to accompany a captain in the carabinieri during an ongoing investigation, but the stakes were high and Jack's hunch seemed as good as any. Besides, Lucca knew Jack, in his day, was probably as good of a detective as he was. Maybe even better. So he was grateful to have Jack seated next to him when the Alitalia A320 landed on the runway in Rome.

Moments later, a carabinieri officer greeted Lucca and Jack at the ramp as they disembarked. The officer seemed nervous.

"I'm afraid I just received disappointing news," the officer explained. "Evelyn Manners was hospitalized two days ago with a heart condition."

"Where is she now?" asked Lucca, pissed he wasn't informed of this earlier.

"The Clinica Mater Dei on Via Antonio Bertoloni. I have a car to take you there if you wish."

"If I wish?" Lucca snapped. "Do you think we came all this way just to chat on a tarmac?"

The officer shook his head sheepishly and escorted them to his car.

AFTER TWO HOURS weaving through midday Roman traffic, the car waited, double-parked and with its lights still flashing, outside the Clinica Mater Dei in the middle of Rome.

The clinic was a private coronary hospital serving the local elite and the odd charity case sponsored by the Vatican.

Jack and Lucca were hustled down a congested corridor by an orderly. Jack eyed geriatric patients strapped to gurneys while Lucca started to grill a nurse at the desk.

After a long interchange in Italian, Lucca turned to Jack unsettled.

"They released Evelyn Manners three hours ago against her doctor's advice."

"Into whose custody?" Jack asked rattled.

"She signed herself out," Lucca replied. "A younger woman picked her up. The nurse didn't get her name but said she was definitely American."

Jack salivated knowing they were close. "The house, Lucca. We gotta check the house!"

Lucca questioned the officer accompanying them. The officer rattled off an address.

The three of them rushed out of the hospital.

Chapter XXIV

The Roman squad car parked down the street from a modest but well-groomed isolated villa on the outskirts of Rome. Lucca climbed out and signaled the officer to watch the perimeter. Jack watched as Lucca unholstered his gun.

"Got an extra one of those?" Jack asked, nodding to it.

Lucca eyed him apprehensively.

"She's three for three, Lucca. I got this nagging aversion to being number four."

Lucca took a moment to consider his request. He confiscated Jack's gun the first time he hauled Jack in as a suspect for Donato's murder. Perhaps, had he let Jack hang onto it, the killer would be dead instead of the other partners.

In any case, he trusted Jack's instincts. Lucca had no idea what they were really up against and what might await them inside the house of Evelyn Manners.

In retrospect, he should've called for back-up. But they were there now and time was running out.

The Transitalia board meeting to ratify the Bremencorp takeover would be starting shortly. If Claudia was inside getting ready for it, an extra gun aimed in her direction might be necessary to take her down.

Lucca pulled a small Glock from the ankle holster on his left leg and handed it to Jack. Jack took it, nodding approvingly.

Lucca and Jack kept out of sight as they approached the house. As they neared it, Lucca split off and headed for the front door while Jack snaked his way around back.

Jack could hear Lucca ringing the front doorbell of the house as he hopped the two-meter stone wall protecting Evelyn Manners' backyard. Once he hit ground, Jack's Glock was at the ready.

THE YARD WAS POPULATED by a bizarre assortment of stone statuary. As Jack wove through them, he noticed each sculpture was *pitted*. As he got closer, he realized the pitting wasn't from the weather. The pitting was from *bullets*. The statues had been set up as a makeshift *target range*. Jack eyed them nervously as he moved toward a rear window of the villa. Reaching it, he peeked inside cautiously.

Please tell me you don't have a dog, he thought, remembering the consequences of his last visit to Bellini's villa. Jack waited a beat just to make sure. He tapped the window softly. Nothing. No dog. Jack took out a credit card and worked the lock on the window. He opened it and climbed inside, spinning terrified as—

A huge *Pit Bull* lunged at him from the living room! The dog knocked Jack back outside where they proceeded to roll on the ground fighting with each other violently. The Pit Bull had his jaws clamped on Jack's leg. Jack groaned in pain.

The Glock had fallen on the ground in the scuffle. He grabbed it and aimed it at the dog's head. But he hesitated. The vicious pooch was only doing his job. Jack didn't have the heart to put a bullet in him.

Instead, Jack grabbed the angry mutt by the back of his head and broke the dog's grip on his leg. He yanked him over to a garbage can and stuffed the dog inside. He slammed down the lid and placed a large boulder on top of it to seal his assailant inside.

Lucca missed the entire fiasco. Inside the

house now, Lucca poked his head out of the window.

"Careful, Jack. A sign out front says she has a dog," Lucca warned.

Jack glared at the can as the Pit Bull barked and bounced around inside it. He then headed for the house.

JACK JOINED UP WITH LUCCA in the villa's main salon. If the yard seemed bizarre, the salon was surreal. The entire place was decorated with *opera costumes, masks* and an eerie assortment of *stage backdrops* and *theatrical props*. Jack and Lucca took it all in.

"I think we broke into the gift shop," Jack said, breaking the silence.

"The whole house is decorated like this. But no sign of Evelyn Manners."

Lucca made his way toward the kitchen while Jack walked over to a large Louis the Fourteenth desk that was gilded in gold.

"Evelyn's no pauper," Jack yelled out to Lucca. "This desk is worth a fortune."

Jack started rummaging through its drawers. He found stacks of old newspaper articles. He inspected a few, discovering each of them were reviews of local operas, concerts, and old movies.

Jack combed through the eclectic mix of memorabilia until he found a *worn leather scrapbook* hidden in its own compartment at the bottom of a drawer. He pulled it out, placed it on top of the desk, and opened it. He stared at its contents, fascinated.

The front of the scrapbook was filled with *old photos of an attractive woman on an opera set* applying make-up to other performers.

Jack flipped to the next page and found an *old handbill* announcing that Mascagni's Cavalleria Rusticana was to be performed in Syracuse, NY

Syracuse, Jack thought. *What was Claudia's fascination with Syracuse?*

Jack looked closer at the handbill. He eyed the credits for the opera. They listed *Alberto Massi* as '*The Soprano*' and *Evelyn* *Manners* as '*Make-up Design.'*

"Evelyn was a make-up artist!" Jack called out to Lucca. "She must've showed Claudia the ropes."

Lucca was in another room down the hall opening the doors to a large armoire. Lucca's eyes widened as he found a cache of weapons inside—*a rifle, a 9mm, and a derringer* mounted behind the door.

"Evelyn showed her more than the ropes,"

Lucca yelled back.

Jack was still flipping through the pages of the scrapbook. More handbills, more clippings. Jack zeroed in on one of them.

It was from the '*Talk of the Town*' section of the Syracuse Herald. Jack removed it from the scrapbook. He held the clipping up to the light and started reading the byline out loud.

SMALL TOWN MAKE-UP ARTIST GOES NEAPOLITAN – EVELYN MANNERS DATES ITALIAN OPERA STAR ALBERTO MASSI

The newspaper clipping was dated April 8, 1985. Jack stared at the name of its author—*Amanda Parks*.

Jack's mind raced as he flipped through more pages. He found pictures of *a younger Evelyn Manners, Evelyn with Alberto Massi in Rome, Evelyn and Alberto on stage in Venice, Alberto and Evelyn with a baby girl in their arms, Evelyn with a young girl ...*

Jack kept flipping through the pages. *More photos of Evelyn, more photos of Evelyn with the same young girl* who was getting older now, almost a teenager.

That's when it hit him—the young girl was

starting to look more and more like *Claudia* ... *Amanda*.

"Jesus ..." Jack gasped.

He turned the page. Another newspaper clipping. It was prominent, taking up the entire page. It was a local Italian newspaper clipping announcing Evelyn and Alberto Massi's break-up. Jack read it out loud, stumbling through the translation.

"Opera star Alberto Massi's career in ruin... Abandons his long-time American mistress leaving her penniless..."

He flipped to the next page. The next clipping was from an Italian newspaper with a black and white photo of *Carlo Bellini* at the altar with a *young, dark-haired beauty in a wedding gown*. It was the *same girl* Jack saw growing up in the earlier photos with Evelyn.

The synapses in Jack's brain were firing at warp speed as he started piecing it all together. He flipped through the rest of the book maniacally. He stopped when he found a thick envelope filled with legal documents in the back.

He pulled out the documents and found a birth certificate. It was from a hospital in New York.

He held it up to the light and read it. The document contained what Jack expected, especially in light of what he previously discovered in the scrapbook, but still, as he read it, its contents took his breath away—

Evelyn Manners gave birth to a baby girl on March 9, 1986.

Jack's eyes zeroed in on the newborn baby's name—*CLAUDIA*.

"Jack, you better get over here!" Lucca yelled out from the other room.

Jack jumped up and rushed down the hallway, his mind working in overdrive, his imagination on fire. "It's all here, Lucca … Jesus, what a mind bender! Where are you?"

"In here," Lucca called out from down the hall. Lucca's voice came from a storage room adjacent to the kitchen.

Jack made his way to it and finally found Lucca standing over a large *horizontal freezer* with its door open. The white light shining up from the open freezer reflected off Lucca's face making him appear rather ghoulish. Lucca started to say something. Jack cut him off

"Claudia is the illegitimate daughter of a second-rate Italian opera singer and a jilted make-up girl from Syracuse!" Jack blurted out as he held up the scrapbook. "Something I'm sure a pretentious society schmuck like Carlo wanted to be kept a secret."

Jack pulled out an old photo of Evelyn and Claudia when they were younger and showed it to Lucca. "This is Evelyn Manners. Only Evelyn isn't Claudia's *friend*, Lucca—Evelyn Manners is Claudia's *mother*!"

"Not anymore, she isn't," Lucca replied as he stared at the freezer beneath them.

Jack leaned over it apprehensively for a look. He gasped, seeing the *body of an old woman covered in ice* inside the freezer. Jack stifled his gag reflex.

Lucca remained calm. "I think we've just met Evelyn Manners."

Jack leaned against the wall trying to recover. He checked his watch, totally amped.

"The board meeting starts in an hour," Jack warned. "Evelyn would have to be represented there… a relative, an attorney, *someone*!"

Lucca nodded and they rushed out of the room.

Still inside the garbage can in the rear yard, the Pit Bull howled violently as Jack and Lucca sped away in the squad car. It was almost as if he was howling a warning. A warning to his owner. A warning to someone with instincts even more violent than his own.

Chapter XXV

The squad car screeched to a stop in front of a modern seven-story office building in downtown Rome. Double-parked, and with the car's lights still flashing, the local officer remained behind as Jack and Lucca raced up the stairs toward the front door of the building. High above them, a squadron of pigeons landed on a balcony. If Jack had the time, he might have wondered if the birds had flown in from Venice to witness the finale of the nightmare that started for him less than a week earlier. But Jack didn't have the time—and his nightmare was far from over.

THE FIFTH FLOOR elevator doors sprang open. Lucca and Jack rushed out of them and sprinted toward the closed doors of a conference room down the hall.

Transitalia's mahogany doors were massive and tall as was the security guard standing outside of them. Lucca flashed his badge and waited impatiently for the guard to inspect it. Jack didn't bother. He swung open the doors and plunged inside.

An elderly Bremencorp executive at a podium stopped mid-sentence seeing Jack burst inside. Lucca finally caught up with him.

Jack and Lucca scanned the board members from both companies who were seated around a long conference table. The looks on the executives' faces ranged from outrage to shock. The two companies' yearly gross when added together probably equaled the entire GDP of Malta. They weren't used to this type of intrusion. And it was particularly unpleasant at this precise moment, as both sides were just getting ready to vote on the merger.

The Bremencorp executive at the podium was the first to compose himself. "Can I help you, gentlemen?" he asked irritated.

Lucca held up his badge. "I'm Captain Lucca Giovanni of the ..."

"Who's representing Evelyn Manners?" Jack yelled, cutting Lucca off.

Lucca felt emasculated, but Jack didn't notice. Or care. He was too busy walking around the room to get a clearer view of the people in attendance.

"No one is representing Mrs. Manners," the

executive at the podium replied impatiently.

"Cut the bullshit!" Jack replied aggravated. "As of two days ago, Evelyn Manners is one of Transitalia's biggest shareholders! She *has* to be represented!"

"Mrs. Manners…" the executive replied petulantly, pointing toward the far end of the conference table, "is representing *herself.*"

Jack spun around and zeroed in on an *old woman* twenty yards away from him at the end of the conference table.

The old woman stayed calm as Jack walked toward her. His eyes squinted from the sun flashing through the windows behind her. As he got closer, he remembered the pictures in the scrapbook. The resemblance was uncanny. The old woman looked *exactly* like Evelyn Manners.

"This is an outrage!" the Bremencorp executive called out angrily from the podium. "Just what is the purpose of this intrusion?"

Jack ignored him. He was ten feet from the woman now. The old woman's eyes darted around the room nervously. Jack wasn't taking any chances. He reached inside his jacket for his Glock.

The old woman finally spooked.

She jumped up from her chair.

The gray wig flew off her head as she whipped out a .38 from her purse and aimed it at Jack!

Jack dove to the ground as *she fired*.

The guard from the front door tackled her from behind.

The crowd screamed and dove to the floor.

Jack jumped across the table and plunged into the fray. He helped the guard fight the woman who was now clawing at them like a leopard, kicking wildly, screaming at the top of her lungs.

Lucca dove in from behind as more carabinieri burst into the conference room, their shrill whistles blowing.

Jack, Lucca, and the guard finally managed to subdue her. They jerked her to her feet. Jack stared repulsed at the mangled, wrinkled make-up and the crazed imposter underneath it.

Claudia looked grotesque.

Her eyes were filled with hatred for the man who just turned her dreams into despair. She spit in Jack's face then jerked herself free and lunged at him. The carabinieri grabbed her and held her back.

Lucca was tired of her antics. "Get her out of here!" he screamed.

A guard handcuffed her from behind as

three more guards yanked her out of the room. As they did, a violent, bloodcurdling scream exploded from Claudia's mouth—

"NNNNNNOOOOOOOOO!!"

A chill tore its way down Jack's spine as they dragged Claudia away.

Chapter XXVI

Claudia's nervous fingers ground a cigarette into an ashtray. It was the only item on the stark white interrogation table in front of her. She was seated behind it in a white smock, her body turned sideways, and her attention fixated on a spider crawling up the wall. Her face was gaunt, her eyes lifeless. Lucca circled her, holding a pencil and pad. He questioned her relentlessly. Her answers were brief, her voice monotone and defiant.

HALF A MILE AWAY, inside Giorgio's office in the Accademia, Jack's voice was equally monotone but absent defiance. His eyes had a lifelessness of their own. The last few days had wounded him body and soul. Giorgio sat across from him as Jack slouched exhausted in a chair eyeing Tintoretto's Cain and Abel, the painting he retrieved for the Gallery a week earlier.

"You were right, Giorgio. Only a *Venetian*

could make murder so beautiful," Jack mused, revisiting Claudia's tactics over and over again in his mind. "She'd always planned to kill the partners by pretending to be Franchesca. But she had one nagging little problem—the carabinieri would always be looking for Franchesca, who, of course, they would never find. So when I stumbled onto the scene, she found the perfect patsy. One she could frame for the murders while she walked away clean. And being alive when everyone else thinks you're dead is about as clean as it gets..."

BACK INSIDE LUCCA'S interrogation room, Claudia's face contorted in anger as Lucca yelled at her for more concise answers. Lucca needed the confession to try to make sense of her crimes.

BUT INSIDE GIORGIO'S OFFICE, Jack proved to be the one to nail Claudia's motives and her plans gone awry.

"Everything worked like a charm," Jack continued, "except her mother dying inconveniently of a heart attack just hours before the meeting. Claudia had no choice but to go herself disguised as her mother. This was easy because her mother was a retired make-up artist, and an amateur marksman, so everything she needed, including a weapon, was inside that house…"

Jack finally straightened in his chair as Giorgio sat across from him mesmerized by the tale.

"She got within ten minutes of a billion dollars, Giorgio. How do you suppose that feels? *One—billion—dollars*."

BACK INSIDE LUCCA'S interrogation room, Claudia watched numbly as Lucca finished scribbling his notes. He was done with her. For now. He didn't get a confession, but there would be more sessions, and he was confident he could break her. By then, she'd have an attorney. Lucca didn't mind. She wasn't going anywhere. He had twenty witnesses who could corroborate the embezzlement charge resulting from the impersonation of her mother. The same witnesses cemented the illegal firearm charge, and the bullet fired at Jack added attempted murder to the list. It would only be a matter of time before he got the murder charges for Franchesca, Donato, Torelli, and Carlo to stick. Claudia was Lucca's first serial killer. Sure, the motive was revenge and money, but if it walks like a duck and talks like a duck… *se-*

rial killer, Lucca thought, staring at her one last time before he left. *Jesus, but she's so beautiful.*

Lucca walked to the metal door and signaled the guard to let him out. As he exited, Claudia stared at the pencil Lucca had unwittingly left behind on the table.

INSIDE GIORGIO'S OFFICE, Jack was standing, getting ready to say good-bye to Giorgio.

"A colleague of mine has a lead on a stolen Titian," Giorgio said, hoping the job prospect would lift Jack's spirits. "He thinks it's in Barcelona. Are you interested?"

Jack stared listlessly out the window into the Grand Canal outside Giorgio's office for a moment. He finally turned back to Giorgio.

"Sure, why not," Jack said, forcing a smile. "I always liked Barcelona. Venice is getting a little damp."

Giorgio stared out the same window as the fog settled on the lagoon. "Legend has it that all our canals were originally filled with tears."

"Whose legend is that?" Jack asked, moved by the metaphor.

"Mine," Giorgio answered, with a wink filled with wisdom older than his years.

Jack smiled warmly. "You're a smart man, Giorgio. I'm gonna miss you."

Jack nodded good-bye and started toward the door. Giorgio called out after him.

"What about Barcelona?"

"Send the details to the hotel," Jack said without turning. With that, he was out the door.

A MILE AWAY, in the same prison cell where Jack was held three days earlier, a guard escorted Claudia to the Spartan cot that was waiting for her. She collapsed, zombie-like, on top of it. She glared at the clues to her case still scribbled in chalk on the walls, realizing who put them there, realizing who put *her* there. She trembled as the guard shut the rusted iron door behind him. She eyed the bars of her cell defiantly. She wouldn't be staying long, this much she knew. She had killed and killing came easy now. It was just a matter of selecting her next victim. Even if the victim turned out to be herself. *She died once before*, she thought. The second time would have to be easier.

Chapter XXVII

Jack climbed out of the motoscafo as it came to rest next to the landing of the Giovanni. He turned toward the other side of the canal hearing someone call out to him.

"Allora, Signor Casanova! How was the amore?"

Jack saw that it was *Paolo*, the gondolier who brought him to the hotel just a few days earlier. All Jack could manage was a half-hearted wave. A smile would have been too much for him. Paolo waved back without smiling. It was almost as if Paolo sensed his innocent greeting cut deep. He began to steer over to the hotel to ask Jack if something was wrong. But he turned, thinking the better of it, as Jack had already disappeared inside the hotel.

ROOM 502 seemed different now. As Jack was packing his luggage, he couldn't help but think that he'd never be returning.

If he returned to anything, he thought, *it should be his marriage*. But he'd done the killing when it came to that one. Still, he wanted to hear Kate's voice. *Was that so selfish?* he thought. Just something, anything to ground him. He was listing precariously in a sea of regret. *Surely, it was okay to call her?*

Jack stopped packing, pulled out his cell phone and dialed. Three rings, which seemed to last forever, then, finally, someone responded.

"Good morning," Kate answered sleepily. It was four a.m. in Manhattan. Kate spoke softly, trying not to wake her sister in the other bedroom. She'd been staying there less than a week, and she didn't want to wear out her welcome.

"Say that with a little more conviction," Jack responded into his cellphone.

"Jack?" Kate said surprised. "Jesus, you scared me yesterday. Are you all right?"

"*All right?* Now that's a loaded question. Hopefully, I can explain why someday. But, yeah, I'm fine. At least, I could be if ..." Jack's voice trailed off. There was an awkward moment of silence. Kate broke it.

"*If* what, Jack?"

Oh, just spit it out, Jack thought. After what

he'd been through, he couldn't believe this would be so difficult for him.

"...*if* maybe you could meet me back in Padua," Jack finally replied.

Kate just hung there a moment, torn, reluctant to respond. Finally, "Meet you for what, Jack?"

"... to help me find the Etruscan. It's a deep canal there, Kate," Jack said flippantly, losing his nerve.

"*Jack!*" she snapped back.

"Look, what do you want from me, Kate? It's been a nightmare here. I just need to see you."

"What's the point?" she said, her bitterness getting the better of her. "We're *over*. You were sure of that, remember?"

"I'm not sure of anything anymore, Kate. I just *need* to see you."

Kate started to break. She didn't want him to hear her crying so she let her anger punch through the tears. "Yeah, right, Jack. Sure—you drive a bulldozer over my heart, shack up with some tramp, then call up a week later and beg to see me! Why, Jack? Goddammit, just tell me why?"

Jack took a long beat. He stared outside at the terrace remembering what took place there.

To answer Kate's question might take years, even an eternity, but he endeavored to try.

"I don't know, Kate. Honest, I don't," he confessed. "I've been chasing fakes and forgeries for so long that sometimes I think I've become one myself. You're about the only thing in my life that's been real. I guess I figure being around you can help get me back on track."

"Well, you'll have to get back on track by yourself, Jack," Kate fired back, "because I'm *retired.*"

"Dammit, Kate, we had ten years!" Jack snapped then he forced himself to calm. "Look, I'm not asking as a husband, okay? I'm asking as a friend."

There was a long silence as Kate struggled with it. She loved him. She never stopped loving him. But no matter how much she wanted to, she could never trust him. Still—she *loved* him. And love, even when you try your best to kill it, is maniacally resilient.

"I'm coming back to Padua in three days to get the rest of my things," she said flatly.

Jack perked. "Then you'll see me?"

"As a *friend*," she answered. "But *only* as a friend. Understand?"

"Understood," Jack said quickly, nodding relieved. Then he heard a click. He frowned.

Wow, she hung up. She could have said more, given me a little something, thrown me a bone, he thought as he pocketed his cellphone. Still, she agreed to come and he was grateful. Everything in Venice now felt foreign to him and he needed *home.*

Jack crossed over to his luggage and zipped up the bag that he was packing before the call. Then he grabbed the room phone and dialed the lobby.

"Bongiorno, this is Jack Sands. Could you send a porter up for my bags?"

"Still in Room 502, signor?" said the clerk in the front lobby who was on the other end of the line.

"Yes. I'm still in Room 502." And, for the first time in his life, Jack couldn't wait to get out of it. He hung up and placed his bags next to the wall near the door. Then he headed outside onto the terrace.

IT WAS ALMOST FIVE and the crimson light that greeted him when he arrived the previous Sunday reappeared on the horizon. Jack took one last look at his favorite sunset, the statues, the topiary, and the marble pond.

Only four days earlier, the most ambiguous part of him thought it found clarity here. Now the clarity was gone. He was drifting again, like the gondolas on the canal beneath him. It was time to get back on land. Real land. Not a city built on the muddy outcrops of a treacherous and ever-changing lagoon.

Jack heard a fluttering of wings. The pigeons had returned. A dozen of them landed on the balustrades above him. He wondered what they came for. Perhaps it was to say goodbye.

Jack was startled by a phone ringing. It was the hotel phone inside the room, and, with its repetitive triple-ring-pause staccato, it seemed to ring with urgency.

After he rushed back inside, Jack finally answered it.

"Yeah?" Jack said into the receiver.

"Jack, it's Lucca," came through the earpiece sharply.

Then there was a loud knock on the door to the room.

"Just a second, Lucca" Jack replied. "The porter's at my door. I'll be right back."

Jack put down the receiver and quickly went to the door. He unlocked it and returned to the phone, calling out to the porter without turning. "My bags are by the door. Careful with the big one."

Jack picked up the phone. "Sorry, Lucca.

What is it?"

Actually, Jack wouldn't have needed to ask the question had he seen the new inmate inside Claudia's cell. It was the prison guard. He was dead. Slumped over the cot. Naked, except for the pencil shoved violently in his eye.

"She's out, Jack!" Lucca replied urgently.

"What? How?" Jack said incredulously.

Before Lucca could answer, Claudia crept up silently behind him. She was wearing the prison guard's uniform and holding the *dagger* from the coat of arms on the wall.

Jack sensed her and spun in shock, as she was ready to strike. Her hand slashed the air. He tried to block it. The blade sliced into his arm. Jack groaned in agony.

She lunged at him. He tackled her and shoved her hard into the wall.

Jack yanked the dagger out of his flesh. She recovered and charged him, jumping on top of him, viciously clawing at his face.

They both went down and struggled violently on the floor. She kicked wildly, ranting and raving like a maniac.

Jack managed to grab both her arms. All the pent up anger and emotion inside him exploded. He pinned her arms behind her back with his knees. She screamed as he grabbed her head and shoved it mercilessly against the floor.

"You wanna die, Claudia!" Jack yelled. "'Cause that's what's next!"

"You don't have the guts, Jack!" she taunted, struggling hard to break his grip. "You'll wimp out. Just like you did in Boston!"

That did it. Jack snapped. He clamped his hands in a vice grip around her neck. His veins bulged with hatred as he tightened his grip.

She gagged, her eyes wide with terror, her face turning blue. Jack was seconds away from a murder rap himself, but something inside him made him stop.

Jack loosened his grip. She gasped for breath. He grabbed her angrily by her hair and kept her head pinned down.

"There's only one thing I can't figure," he said panting, spent. "How did you kill Franchesca?!"

She didn't answer. He yanked her head up by her hair and shoved it back down hard on the marble. "Goddammit, talk to me!"

She almost passed out from the pain. Claudia's mind drifted back to that rainy night at the Fish Market. Claudia had stalked her as Franchesca ran to get out of the rain. Claudia remembered how much she hated wearing the mask and that ridiculous cape. But it worked. Franchesca never knew who murdered her that night. Who attacked her from behind. Who shoved the plastic bag over her face. Who held it there, tightening it, until she suffocated. Claudia remembered how badly she wanted to kill Franchesca from afar with a bullet, like she used later with Carlo and Torelli. She was nervous about her first kill being so *up close and personal*. But she needed Franchesca's body to be clean. The coroner would have noticed stab marks or a gunshot wound, even on a charred body. No, Claudia needed Franchesca's corpse clean to pull off the switch. And she almost *did* pull it off—if it weren't for the animal who now had her pinned to the floor.

Jack yanked her head back up and slammed it down again, screaming, "Answer me! How did you kill Franchesca?"

Claudia clenched her teeth angrily. "I followed her one night," she finally answered, glaring at him. "Strangled her in the rain. She was pitiful. She was weak. She never even put up a fight."

Jack was repulsed. He stared at her as if she were an alien. His mind raced trying to piece the rest of it together. He yanked her hair again.

"How did you get her into the room?" he yelled. "The passage? Is that how you did it?! The same way you got in here now?!"

A sick, perverse smile came over Claudia's face as she stared at the *large antique armoire* hovering above them.

And then it hit him, Jack finally put it together.

"Jesus, the *armoire*—you hid Franchesca's body inside the *armoire*!"

Jack flashed back to the first time he saw Claudia. She was in the Motoscafo with the armoire heading toward the Giovanni. It was brilliant. It was never philanthropy—she restored a few pieces for the hotel because she needed to get Franchesca's body inside the room without anyone knowing. And the armoire was the only thing the body would fit in.

Jack was so shocked by her scheme's perfection that he eased up on his grip.

Bad move. She broke free and wrestled out from under him, grabbing a statue from the table.

Jack lunged at her, but she swung the statue hard. It smashed into the top of his head.

The blow sent him crashing through the window and out onto the terrace.

He landed with a thud on the edge of the

marble pond. He was dazed. He struggled to stand.

Relentless, she barreled toward him. He threw up his hands to protect himself as she rushed him with the statue, screaming, "You took everything, Jack!"

She smashed the statue mercilessly across his head a second time. Jack plunged backward to the ground while she hovered over him, numb, almost catatonic.

"I spent years with a pig to get my share!" she yelled. "I earned it! I wasn't going to end up like my mother. But you took it away ... *YOU TOOK IT AWAY!"*

She struck him hard again as he turned away from her. The statue crashed into his back bursting into a hundred pieces. He groaned in agony as the blow sent him into the balustrades on the edge of the terrace.

She bent down and picked up another statue, a *winged lion.* Her adrenaline was pumping hard. The thing must have weighed fifty pounds. Jack was out of it, he didn't even see her.

"There's just one thing you didn't count on," she said, standing in front of him, ready to crush him with the statue. "You see, Jack, you and I are different. *I don't bend over!"*

Then she lifted the statue high over her head with almost super-human strength. "Good-bye, Jack," she murmured icily. Then she rushed him with the statue ready to crush him.

Jack's eyes struggled to focus. His muscles strained to move.

As she flew into him ready to shatter his skull, Jack finally reacted.

He buried his foot in her stomach as he fell backward, stiffening his leg, and, using her forward momentum, he jerked his leg upward *hard* and catapulted her over the terrace!

Fifty feet below, on the Grand Canal beneath them, the statue hit first, followed by the twisting, turning, *screaming* body of Claudia as she plunged into the icy water of the lagoon.

Her arms flailed underwater, finally forcing herself to the surface where she coughed violently, gasping for breath.

Claudia turned horrified hearing the rapid drone of a whistle, spotting—

A *Vaporetto* heading straight toward her!

The Captain of the lumbering steel water-bus had no time to react. He jerked the wheel. Too late.

The passengers screamed hearing a *thud* on the hull as the vaporetto crashed over the top of her.

The captain was beside himself. He finally stopped the boat. The passengers raced back to the stern to look for her body.

But it never surfaced.

The passengers stared horrified at the violent whirlpool of white foam churning around the prop as it suddenly turned *blood red.*

Chapter XXVIII

It was early dawn. The costumed crowds were still in their beds, the carnival itself sleeping with them. Soon they would awaken. The ancient city waited serenely for the onslaught.

Jack stared at the empty colonnades and the lonely gondolas bobbing in their slips as his motoscafo pulled away from the dock on the Piazza San Marco. He sat alone in the back with his luggage, badly bruised and badly shaken.

As the motoscafo churned through the icy waters of the lagoon, Jack opened a letter. It was just a single, handwritten page addressed to him from Lucca. It fluttered in the breeze as he read it.

Dear Jack,
On behalf of Venice, I apologize for everything we've put you through. As I promised, I'll call when we recover the body. But keep in mind, the canals are deep and the currents are treacherous

this time of year. Things tend to get lost
in them. You certainly did.
Ciao, Jack—Lucca.

Jack looked out over the motoscafo's wake and held the letter up to the wind. He released it. It sailed a few meters before falling onto the water. After a moment or two, it disappeared beneath the foaming wake.

Jack soberly watched the most seductive view in the world recede away. The winged lion perched on a column above the Piazza San Marco with its pigeons feeding on the ground beneath it was a spectacle that billions cherished. *The city where lions fly and pigeons walk*, he remembered Rossini musing.

Well, the pigeons and lions can have her, Jack thought. He had seen the last of her.

He turned his back on the siren-like city and stared ahead at the mainland as the motoscafo sped away from the lagoon.

Chapter XXIX

The olive trees gently whipped past as Jack drove down the narrow highway toward Padua. He was back inside his vintage '65 Alfa Romeo Giulia ragtop. It had been safely tucked away in the parking lot near the train station in Mestre. The Alfa's leather seat hugged him warmly. He was grateful to be behind the wheel again. On land. On the open road. Away from anything liquid.

JACK ARRIVED BACK IN PADUA without notice and without fanfare. At least he could take solace in that. He'd had his fill of *reporters*.

The Alfa pulled up in front of his country villa. There wasn't any parking in front, so he drove into a small lot near the field across the street. He turned off the Alfa's throaty engine and took a moment to bask in the Paduan stillness. The sweet smell of mulberry trees and the fresh country air were tonic for his gloom.

Jack climbed out and walked past some children playing near a beggar. As was his habit, he generously dropped some euros into the beggar's basket.

He eyed his small villa thirty meters away and smiled relieved seeing Kate coming down its front stairs. Kate stopped, torn and reluctant, as she reached the street. But as he drew closer, seeing his bruises and the pain in his eyes, she found herself moving toward him.

Jack's nervous hand found hers. He held it a moment, staring, beaten and confused, into her eyes. Kate finally relented. She allowed him, awkwardly, gratefully, to find comfort in her arms.

The children smiled as they watched them from the road. The leaves in the mulberry trees rustled above them as they played and pranced past the beggar.

But the beggar wasn't smiling.

As Jack and Kate disappeared inside their Paduan villa, the beggar turned and walked away.

She removed the tattered shawl from over her head and revealed an unexpected but familiar face— it was the *chambermaid* from the Palazzo Giovanni.

The chambermaid quickly crossed the dirt

road behind the villa and climbed into the driver's seat of a car that was parked forty meters away.

She whispered something to a *passenger* waiting in the back seat. Then she turned, started the engine, and put the car in gear.

As the car pulled away, the passenger in the back seat stared through the rear window at the villa as Jack and Kate climbed, hand in hand, up its stairs.

The dancing shadows from the trees above the car reflected in the glass obscuring the passenger's *heavily bandaged face*. It seemed like fresh traces of blood were still bleeding into the gauze.

One thing bleeding for certain, however, was the hatred out of the passenger's dark, tortured, revenge-filled eyes as she watched Kate and Jack disappear inside the villa.

They look so happy, Claudia thought. And she contented herself with making the plans to change that as the car sped away.

JACK SANDS WILL RETURN IN

ROOM 503

.

ABOUT THE AUTHOR

Kevin Alyn Elders is an Author, Screenwriter, Producer and Director living in the Pacific Northwest and Villefranche Sur Mer. From his early works, including the *Iron Eagle* action adventure series, through his later works, including *Echelon Conspiracy*, he has written in many genres. His taut, compelling, suspense-filled narratives have found their latest incarnation in his Screen Novel Series of Paperbacks, Ebooks and Audio Books.

Join his Insider Readers List for Special Offers:
www.Kevinalynelders.com/mail/?p=subscribe

Author's Website:
www.KevinAlynElders.com

Follow him on Facebook:
www.Facebook.com/KevinAlynElders

For a list of his Theatrical work:
https://www.imdb.com/name/nm0253106/

Also by the Author

The Immaculate

Room 503

Rubicon

Fate of A Nation

The Dark Prophet